you know you love me
ᵃ gossip girl
novel

gossip girl **novels by Cecily von Ziegesar:**

Gossip Girl

You Know You Love Me

All I Want Is Everything

you know you love me
a gossip girl
novel

by
Cecily von Ziegesar

LITTLE, BROWN AND COMPANY
New York ☞ An AOL Time Warner Company

First Edition

The characters and events in this book are fictitious. Any similarity to real persons, living or dead, is coincidental and not intended by the author.

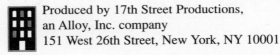 Produced by 17th Street Productions,
an Alloy, Inc. company
151 West 26th Street, New York, NY 10001

Library of Congress Cataloging-in-Publication Data

Von Ziegesar, Cecily.
   You know you love me : a Gossip Girl novel / by Cecily von Ziegesar.
— 1st ed. p. cm.
   Summary: Blair and Serena, who go to an exclusive private school in Manhattan, are no longer best friends but are still both consumed with thoughts of boyfriends and college.
   ISBN 0-316-70149-1
   [1. New York (N.Y.) — Fiction. 2. High schools — Fiction. 3. Schools — Fiction.] I. Title.

PZ7.V94 Yo 2002
[Fic] — dc21

                                                              2002066087

10 9 8 7 6 5 4 3 2 1
COM-MO
Printed in the United States of America

you know you love me

I'm your Venus, I'm your fire. At your desire.
—Bananarama, "Venus"

hey people!

Welcome to New York City's Upper East Side, where my friends and I all live in huge, fabulous apartments and go to exclusive private schools. We aren't always the nicest people in the world, but we make up for it in looks and taste.

Winter is coming. It's the city's favorite season and mine, too. The boys are out in Central Park, playing ball or doing whatever boys do this time of year, getting all mussed up with bits of dried leaves on their sweaters and in their hair. And those pink cheeks . . . talk about irresistible!

It's time to break out those credit cards and hit Bendel's and Barneys for some cool new boots, sexy fishnet tights, little wool skirts, and delicious cashmere sweaters. The city feels a little sparklier this time of year, and we want to sparkle with it!

Unfortunately, it's also time to fill out our college applications. We all come from the sorts of families and go to the sorts of schools where not applying to the Ivy Leagues is not an option, and not getting into them would be a total embarrassment. The pressure is on, but I refuse to let it get to me. This is our senior year of high school and we're going to live it up and make our mark and still get into the colleges of our choice. We've got the finest blood on the East Coast—I'm sure we can figure out how to have our cake and eat it too, just as we always have.

I know a few girls who aren't going to let the pressure get them down. . . .

Sightings

B with her dad, shopping for sunglasses in **Gucci** on Fifth Avenue. He couldn't decide on the pink tinted lenses or the baby blue so he bought them both. Wow, he really is gay! **N** and his pals looking up the best party schools in the *Insider's Guide to Colleges* at **Barnes & Noble** on 86th and Lexington. **S** getting a facial at **Aveda** downtown. And **D**, dreamily watching the ice-skaters in **Rockefeller Center** and writing in a notebook. A poem about **S** no doubt—what a romantic. Also, **B** getting a Brazilian wax at the **J. Sisters Salon**. Prepping herself for . . .

IS *B* REALLY READY TO TAKE THE NEXT STEP?

She's been talking about it ever since summer ended and she and **N** were back in the city, together again. Then **S** showed up, **N**'s eyes began to wander, and **B** decided to punish him by making him wait. But now **S** has **D,** and **N** has promised to stay faithful to **B.** It's time. After all, no one really wants to go to college a virgin.

I'll be watching closely.

You know you love me,

gossip girl

having her cake and losing it, too

"To my Blair Bear," Mr. Harold Waldorf, Esq. said, raising his glass of champagne to clink it against Blair's. "You're still my little girl, even though you wear leather pants and have a hunky boyfriend." He flashed a suntanned smile at Nate Archibald, who was seated beside Blair at the small restaurant table. Mr. Waldorf had chosen Le Giraffe for their special dinner because it was small and intimate and trendy, the food was fabulous, and the waiters all had the sexiest French accents.

Blair Waldorf reached under the tablecloth and squeezed Nate's knee. The candlelight was making her horny. *If only Daddy knew what we're planning to do after this,* she thought giddily. She clinked glasses with her father and took a giant gulp of champagne.

"Thanks, Daddy," she said. "Thanks for coming all this way just to visit me."

Mr. Waldorf put his glass down and patted his lips dry with his napkin. His fingernails were shiny and perfectly manicured. "Oh, I didn't come for you, darling. I came here to show off." He cocked his head to one side and pursed his lips like a model posing for a picture. "Don't I look great?"

Blair dug her fingernails into Nate's leg. She had to admit

her father *did* look great. He had lost about twenty pounds, he was tan, he was wearing gorgeous French clothes, and he seemed happy and relaxed. Still, she was glad he'd left his boyfriend at home in their château in France. She wasn't quite ready to see her father engaged in public displays of affection with another man, no matter how good he looked.

She picked up her menu. "Can we order?"

"I'm having steak," Nate announced. He didn't want to make a big fuss over what he was having. He just wanted to get this dinner over with. Not that he minded hanging out with Blair's flaming father: it was actually kind of entertaining to see how gay he'd become. But Nate was anxious to get back to Blair's house. She was finally going to give it up. And it was about time.

"Me too," Blair said, closing her menu without really looking at it. "Steak." She didn't plan on eating much anyway, not tonight. Nate had promised her he was completely over Serena van der Woodsen, Blair's classmate and former best friend. He was ready to give Blair his undivided attention. She didn't care whether she ate steak or mussels or brains for dinner—she was finally going to lose her virginity!

"Me three," said her father. "Trois steak au poivre," he told the waiter in a perfect French accent. "And the name of the person who cuts your hair. You have marvelous hair."

Blair's cheeks flamed. She grabbed a bread stick from the basket on the table and bit into it. Her father's voice and mannerisms were completely different from when she'd seen him nine months ago. Then, he'd been a conservative, suit-wearing lawyer, all clean lines and sharp edges. Perfectly respectable. Now he was totally camp, with his plucked eyebrows and lavender shirt and matching socks. It was so embarrassing. After all, he was her *dad*.

Last year, Blair's father's coming out and her parents' ensuing divorce had been the talk of the town. Now everyone was pretty much over it, and Mr. Waldorf was free to show his handsome face wherever he pleased. But that wasn't to say that the other diners at Le Giraffe weren't taking notice. They definitely were.

"Did you see his socks?" an aging heiress whispered to her bored husband. *"Pink-and-gray argyle."*

"Think he's got enough crap in his hair? Who does he think he is, anyway? Brad Pitt?" a famous lawyer asked his wife.

"He's got a better figure than his ex-wife, I'll tell you that much," one of the waiters remarked.

It was all very amusing, to everyone except Blair. Sure, she wanted her father to be happy, and it was okay for him to be gay. But did he have to be so obvious about it?

Blair looked out the window at the streetlights twinkling in the crisp November air. Smoke billowed out of chimneys on the roofs of the luxurious townhouses across Sixty-fifth Street.

Finally their salads came.

"So it's still Yale for next year?" Mr. Waldorf said, as he stabbed at a piece of endive. "That's where you've got your heart set on going, right, Bear? My old alma mater?"

Blair put her salad fork down and sat back in her chair, leveling her pretty blue eyes at her father. "Where else would I go?" she said, as if Yale University were the only college on the planet.

Blair didn't understand why people applied to six or seven colleges, some of them so bad they were called "safeties." She was one of the best students in the senior class at the Constance Billard School for Girls, a small, elite, all-girls, uniforms-required school on East Ninety-third Street. All Constance's girls went to good colleges. But Blair never settled for just plain good. She had to have the best of everything, no compromises. And the best college, in her opinion, was Yale.

Her father laughed. "So I guess those other colleges like Harvard and Cornell should send you letters of apology for even trying to get you to go to them, huh?"

Blair shrugged and examined her newly manicured finger-nails. "I just want to go to Yale, that's all."

Her father glanced at Nate, but Nate was looking around for something else to drink. He hated champagne. What he really wanted was a beer, even though it never seemed appropriate to order one in a place like Le Giraffe. They always made such a fuss about it, bringing you a cold frosted glass and then pouring in the Heineken like it was something special, when it was just the same old crap you could get at a basketball game.

"What about you, Nate?" Mr. Waldorf asked. "Where are you applying?"

Blair was already nervous about losing her virginity. All this talk about college was just making things worse. She pushed her chair back and stood up to go to the bathroom. She knew it was disgusting and that she had to learn to stop, but whenever she got nervous, she made herself throw up. It was her only bad habit.

Actually, that's not exactly true. But we'll get to that later.

"Nate's going to Yale with me," she told her father. Then she turned and strode confidently through the restaurant.

Nate watched her go. She looked hot in her new black silk halter top, with her straight, dark brown hair hanging between her bare shoulder blades, and her skintight leather pants hugging her hips. She looked like she had already done it, many times.

Leather pants tend to have that effect.

"So it's going to be Yale for you, too?" Mr. Waldorf prompted when Blair had gone.

Nate frowned at his champagne glass. He really, really wanted a beer. And he really, really didn't think he could get into Yale. You can't wake and bake and take a calculus test and expect to get into Yale—you just can't. And that was what he'd been doing lately. A lot.

"I'd *like* to go to Yale," he said. "But I think Blair's going to be disappointed. I mean, my grades just aren't that good."

Mr. Waldorf winked at him. "Well, just between you and me, I think Blair's being a little hard on all the other schools in the country. No one says you have to go to Yale. There are plenty of other schools out there."

Nate nodded. "Yeah. Brown seems pretty cool. I have an interview there next weekend," he said. "Although that's definitely going to be a stretch, too. I got a C on my last math test, and I'm not even taking the AP," he admitted. "Blair doesn't think Brown is even a real school. You know, because they have less requirements, or whatever."

"Blair has impossibly high standards," Mr. Waldorf said. He sipped his champagne, his buffed pinky pointing outward. "She takes after me."

Nate glanced sideways at the other diners in the restaurant. He wondered if they thought he and Mr. Waldorf were together, boyfriends. To squelch such speculation, he pushed up the sleeves of his green cashmere sweater and cleared his throat in a very manly way. Blair had given him the sweater last year, and he'd been wearing it a lot lately to reassure her that he wasn't about to break up with her or cheat on her or do whatever it was she was worried about. "I don't know," he said, grabbing a roll from the bread basket and breaking it violently in half. "It would be great to just take a year off and go sailing with my dad or something, you know?"

Nate didn't understand why, at seventeen, you had to map out your entire life. There would be plenty of time for more school after taking a year or two off to sail around the Caribbean or go skiing in Chile. And yet, all of his classmates at the St. Jude's School for Boys were planning to go straight to college and straight to grad school after college. The way Nate saw it, they were signing their lives away without thinking about what they really wanted to do. For example, he loved the sound of the cold Atlantic spraying against the bow of his boat. He loved the feel of the hot sun on his back as he hoisted the sails. He loved the way the sun flashed green before it dropped into the ocean. Nate figured there had to be more stuff out there like that, and he wanted to experience it, all of it.

As long as it didn't require too much effort. He wasn't big on making an effort.

"Well, Blair's not going to be happy when she finds out you're thinking of taking time off." Mr. Waldorf chuckled. "You're supposed to go to Yale together and get married and live happily ever after."

Nate's eyes followed Blair as she walked back to the table, her head held high. All the other diners in the restaurant were watching her, too. She wasn't the best-dressed or the skinniest or the tallest girl in the room, but she seemed to sparkle a bit more brightly than the rest of them. And she knew it.

Their steaks came and Blair tore into hers, washing it down with gulps of champagne and mounds of buttery mashed potatoes. She watched the sexy way Nate's temple throbbed as he chewed. She couldn't wait to get out of there. She couldn't wait to finally do it with the boy she was planning to spend the rest of her life with. It couldn't get more right than that.

Nate couldn't help noticing how intensely Blair was wielding her steak knife. She cut the meat into huge hunks and gnawed on them ferociously. It made him wonder if she'd be that intense in bed. They'd fooled around a lot, but he'd always been the more aggressive one. Blair always just kind of lay there, making the sorts of mewing sounds girls made in the movies, while he roamed around, doing things to her. But tonight Blair seemed impatient, *hungrier*.

Of course she was hungry. She'd just thrown up.

"They don't serve food like this at Yale, Bear," Mr. Waldorf told his daughter. "You'll be eating pizza and Combos in the dorms with the rest of them."

Blair wrinkled her nose. She'd never eaten a Combo in her life. "No way," she said. "Nate and I aren't going to live in a dorm, anyway. We're going to have our own place." She stroked Nate's ankle with the toe of her boot. "I'll learn how to cook."

Mr. Waldorf raised his eyebrows at Nate. "Lucky you," he joked.

Nate grinned and licked the mashed potatoes off his fork. He wasn't about to tell Blair that her little dream of them living in an off-campus apartment together in New Haven was even more absurd than the idea of her eating Combos. But he didn't want to say anything to upset her.

"Shut up, Daddy," said Blair.

The plates were cleared. Impatient, Blair twisted her little ruby ring around and around on her finger. She shook her head to coffee and dessert and stood up to head for the ladies' room once more. Twice in one meal was extreme, even for her, but she was so nervous she couldn't help it.

Thank goodness Le Giraffe had nice, private bathrooms.

When Blair came out again, the entire waitstaff filed out of the kitchen. The maître d' was holding a cake decorated with flickering candles. Eighteen of them, including one extra for luck.

Oh God.

Blair stomped back to the table in her pointy stiletto boots and took her seat, glaring at her father. Why did he have to make a scene? It wasn't her fucking birthday for another three weeks. She downed another glass of champagne in one gulp.

Waiters and cooks surrounded the table. And then the singing began.

"Happy birthday to you . . ."

Blair grabbed Nate's hand and squeezed it tight. "Make them stop," she whispered.

But Nate just sat there grinning like an asshole. He kind of liked it when Blair was embarrassed. It didn't happen very often.

Her father was more sympathetic. When he saw how miserable Blair was he increased the tempo and quickly finished the song. *"You smell like a monkey, and you look like one too!"*

The waitstaff clapped politely and went back to their posts.

"I know it's a little early," Mr. Waldorf said apologetically. "But I have to leave tomorrow, and seventeen is such a big birthday. I didn't think you'd mind."

Mind? No one likes to be sung to in public. *No one.*

Silently Blair blew out the candles and examined the cake. It was elaborately decorated with marzipan high-heeled shoes walking down a spun-sugar Fifth Avenue, past a rock-candy model of Henri Bendel, her favorite store. It was exquisite.

"For my little shoe fetishista," her father said, beaming. He pulled a wrapped present out from under the table and handed it to Blair.

Blair shook the box, expertly recognizing the hollow, thudding sound that a pair of new shoes makes when they're shaken in their box. She tore into the paper. MANOLO BLAHNIK, said the type in big bold letters on the lid of the box. Blair held her breath and pulled off the lid. Inside was a pair of beautifully crafted pewter leather mules with adorable little kitten heels.

Très fabulous.

"I got them in Paris," Mr. Waldorf said. "They only made a few hundred pairs. I bet you're the only girl in town who has them."

"They're fantastic," Blair breathed.

She stood up and walked around the table to hug her father. The shoes made up for him humiliating her in public. Not only were they unbelievably cool, but they were exactly what she was going to wear later that night when she and Nate had sex. Those and nothing else.

Thanks, Daddy!

what the steps of the metropolitan museum of art are really for

"Let's sit in the back," Serena van der Woodsen said as she led Daniel Humphrey into Serendipity 3 on East Sixtieth Street. The narrow, old-timey hamburger-and–ice cream parlor was crowded with parents treating their kids while the nanny took the night off. The air was punctuated with the shrill cries of sugared-up children, as tired waitresses hurried to and fro carrying huge glass bowls of ice cream, frozen hot chocolates, and extralong hot dogs.

Dan had planned to go somewhere more romantic with Serena. Somewhere quiet and dimly lit. Somewhere where they could hold hands and talk and get to know each other without being distracted by angry parents scolding deceptively angelic-looking little boys in button-down shirts and khakis from Brooks Brothers. But Serena had wanted to come here.

Maybe she was really craving ice cream, or maybe her expectations for the evening weren't quite as big and romantic as his were.

"Isn't this great?" she burbled exuberantly. "Me and my brother, Erik, used to come here like once a week and eat peppermint sundaes." She picked up a menu and examined it. "It's still all exactly the same. I love it."

Dan smiled and shook the scraggly brown hair out of his eyes. The truth was, he didn't really care where he was, as long as he was with her.

Dan was from the West Side, and Serena was from the East. He lived with his father, a self-proclaimed intellectual and the editor of lesser-known Beat poets, and his little sister, Jenny, who was in ninth grade at Constance Billard, the same school Serena went to. They lived in a crumbling Upper West Side apartment that hadn't been renovated since the 1940s. The only person who did any cleaning around the place was their huge cat, Marx, who was an expert at killing and eating cock-roaches. Serena lived with her well-heeled parents, who were on the board of just about every big institution in the city, in an enormous penthouse decorated by a famous decorator, with a view of the Metropolitan Museum of Art and Central Park. She had a maid and a cook who she could ask to bake her a cake or make her a cappuccino any time she wanted.

So what was she doing with Dan?

They had stumbled into each other a few weeks ago while trying out for parts in a film directed by Dan's friend and Serena's classmate, Vanessa Abrams. Serena hadn't gotten the part, and Dan had almost given up hope of ever seeing her again, but then they'd met again at a bar in Brooklyn. They'd seen each other and talked on the phone a few times since then, but this was their first real date.

Serena had come back to the city last month after being kicked out of boarding school. At first, she'd been thrilled to be back in the city. But then she'd discovered that Blair Waldorf and all her other old friends had decided not to be friends with her anymore. Serena still didn't know what she'd done that was so awful. Sure, she hadn't really kept in touch with anyone, and sure, she'd maybe bragged a little too much about all the fun she'd had in Europe this past summer. So much fun that she hadn't returned in time for the first day of classes at Hanover Academy in New Hampshire. The school had refused to take her back.

Her old school, Constance Billard, was more forgiving. Well, the *school* was. The girls were not. Serena didn't have a single friend in New York anymore, so she was thrilled to meet Dan. It was fun getting to know someone so different from herself.

Dan wanted to pinch himself every time he looked into Serena's dark blue eyes. He had been in love with her since he first laid eyes on her at a party in ninth grade, and it was his hope that now, two-and-a-half years later, she was falling in love with him, too.

"Let's get the biggest sundaes on the menu," Serena said. "We can switch bowls halfway through so we don't get bored."

She ordered the triple peppermint sundae with extra hot-fudge sauce, and he ordered a coffee banana split. Dan would eat anything with coffee in it. Or tobacco.

"So," Serena said, pointing at the paperback sticking out of Dan's coat pocket, "is that good?"

The book was *No Exit*, by Jean Paul Sartre, an existentialist tale of misfits in purgatory.

"Yeah. It's kind of funny and kind of depressing," Dan said. "But there's a lot of truth to it, I guess."

"What's it about?"

"Hell."

Serena laughed. "Whoa," she said. "Do you always read books like that?"

Dan extracted an ice cube from his water glass and put it in his mouth. "Like what?"

"Like, about hell," she said.

"No, not always." He had just finished reading *The Sorrows of Young Werther,* which was about love. And hell.

Dan liked to think of himself as a tormented soul. He preferred novels and plays and books of poetry that revealed the tragic absurdity of life. They were the perfect accompaniment to coffee and cigarettes.

"I have trouble reading," Serena confessed.

Their sundaes came. They could barely see each other over the mounds of ice cream. Serena dipped her long sundae spoon into the bowl and carved out a perfectly enormous bite. Dan marveled at the long, slim angle of her wrist, the taut muscle of her arm, the golden brilliance of her pale blond hair. She was about to pig out on a disgustingly huge sundae, but to him she was a goddess.

"I mean, I can read, obviously," Serena continued. "I just have trouble paying attention. My mind wanders, and I think about what I'm going to do that night. Or something I need to buy at the drugstore. Or something funny that happened like, a year ago or something." She swallowed the bite of ice cream and looked into Dan's understanding brown eyes. "I just have no attention span," she said sadly.

This was what Dan loved most about Serena. She had the ability to be sad and happy at the same time. She was like a lone angel, floating above the surface of the earth, laughing with delight because she could fly but crying out of loneliness. Serena turned everything ordinary into something extraordinary.

Dan's hands shook as he cut off the tip of his chocolate-covered banana with his spoon and ate it silently. He wanted to tell Serena that he'd read for her. That he'd do anything for her. Coffee ice cream melted and spilled over the edge of his bowl. Dan tried to keep his heart in his chest.

"I had a great English teacher at Riverside last year," he said when he'd regained control. "He told us the best way to retain what you read is to just read a little bit at a time. Savor the words."

Serena loved the way Dan talked. The way he said things made her want to remember them. She smiled and licked her lips. "Savor the words," she repeated, the corners of her mouth curving up into a smile.

Dan swallowed a piece of his banana whole and reached for his water. God, she was beautiful.

"So, you're probably, like, a total A student and you've already applied to Harvard early or something, right?" Serena said. She picked a broken piece of candy cane out of her sundae and sucked on it.

"No way," Dan said. "I'm totally clueless. I mean, I definitely want to go somewhere with a good writing program, I just don't know where yet. Our college advisor gave me this big long list, and I've got all the catalogs, but I still don't know what I'm doing."

"Me neither. But I'm probably going up to visit Brown sometime soon," Serena told him. "My brother goes there. Want to come?"

Dan searched the deep wells of her eyes, trying to gauge whether she felt as passionate about him as he did about her. When she said, "Want to come?" did she mean, "Let's spend the weekend together, holding hands, staring into each other's eyes, and kissing for hours at a time"? Or did she mean, "Let's go together because it would be convenient and fun to have a friend along"? Still, he couldn't say no. He didn't care whether she'd said Brown or Loserville Community College, Serena had asked him if he wanted to go and the answer was yes. He'd go anywhere with her.

"Brown," Dan said, as if he were still thinking it over. "They're supposed to have a great writing program."

Serena nodded, combing her long blond hair with her fingers. "So come with me."

Oh, he'd go. Of course he'd go. Dan shrugged. "I'll talk to my dad about it," he said, trying to sound casual. He didn't dare let Serena know that inside he was leaping and bounding around like an excited puppy. He was afraid he might scare her away.

"Okay, ready? Let's switch," Serena said, pushing her bowl toward Dan.

They switched bowls and tasted each other's sundaes. As soon as the new flavors hit their taste buds, their faces contorted and they stuck out their tongues. Peppermint and coffee didn't mix. Dan hoped it wasn't a sign.

Serena took her bowl back and dug in for the final stretch. Dan took a few more bites of his and then put his spoon down.

"Whoa," he said, leaning back in his chair and clutching his stomach. "You win."

Her bowl was still half full, but Serena put her spoon down, too, and unbuttoned the top button of her jeans. "I think we're tied," she said with a giggle.

"Want to take a walk?" Dan ventured, crossing his trembling fingers and toes so tightly that they turned blue.

"I'd love to," Serena replied.

Sixtieth Street was quiet for a Friday night. They walked west, toward Central Park. At Madison, they stopped at Barneys and looked in the window. There were still a few people behind the counters in the cosmetics department, setting up for the Saturday morning rush.

"I don't know what I'd do without Barneys." Serena sighed, as if the store had saved her life.

Dan had only been inside the famous department store once. He'd let his imagination run wild and had bought a very expensive designer tuxedo there with his father's credit card, fantasizing about wearing it while dancing with Serena at a glamorous party. But then reality had set in. He hated glamorous parties, and until a few days ago, he'd thought Serena would never have two words to say to him. So he'd returned the tux.

Now he smiled at the memory. Serena definitely had more than two words to say to him. She'd invited him to spend the weekend with her. They were falling in love. Maybe they'd even wind up going to the same college and spending the rest of their lives together.

Careful, Dan. There goes that imagination again.

At Fifth Avenue, near the corner of the park, they headed uptown past the Pierre Hotel, where they had both gone to a formal dance in tenth grade. Dan remembered watching Serena, wishing he knew her, as she laughed with her table of friends, dressed in a green, strapless dress that made her hair shimmer. He had been in love with her even then.

They walked past Serena's orthodontist's office and the Frick, the old mansion that was now a museum. Dan wanted to break in and kiss Serena on top of one of the beautiful old beds inside. He wanted to live there with her, like refugees in paradise.

They kept walking up Fifth Avenue, past Blair Waldorf's building on Seventy-second Street. Serena gazed up at it. She'd known Blair since first grade and had been in the Waldorfs' apartment hundreds of times, but now she was no longer welcome.

Serena couldn't pretend she was entirely blameless. She knew what had upset Blair most. It wasn't just that Serena had been out of touch with her old New York crowd or that she'd been off partying in Europe while Blair's parents were getting a divorce. What had really turned their friendship sour was the fact that Serena and Nate had slept together the summer before Serena went away to boarding school.

That was nearly two years ago, and Serena felt like it had happened to some other girl with an entirely different life. Serena, Blair, and Nate had been such a close threesome. Serena had hoped Blair would see it as one of those crazy things that happened between friends and forgive her. It was just a one-off. And besides, Blair still had Nate. But Blair had only recently found out about it, and she wasn't going to let it go.

Serena fished around in her purse for a cigarette and stuck one in her mouth. She stopped walking and flicked on her lighter. Dan waited as she inhaled and blew a cloud of gray smoke into the chilly air. She pulled her worn, brown plaid Burberry coat around her.

"Let's go sit out in front of the Met for a while," she said. "Come on." She took Dan's hand and they quickly covered the ten blocks to the Metropolitan Museum of Art. Serena led Dan halfway up the steps and sat down. Across the street was her apartment building. As usual, her parents were out, attending some charity function or art opening, and the windows were dark and lonely looking.

Serena let go of Dan's hand, and he wondered if he'd done something wrong. He couldn't read her mind, and it was driving him crazy.

"Me and Blair and Nate used to sit on these steps for hours and just talk about nothing," Serena told him wistfully. "Sometimes we were supposed to go out and Blair and I would get all dressed and put on makeup and everything. Then Nate would show up with a bottle of something and we'd buy cigarettes and just ditch the party and sit out here." She looked up at the stars with big, shining eyes. There were tears in them.

"Sometimes I wish . . ." Serena's voice trailed off. She didn't know exactly what she wished, but she was tired of feeling bad about Blair and Nate. "Sorry," she sniffed, looking down at her shoes. "I hope I'm not bumming you out."

"You're not," Dan said.

He wanted to take her hand back, but she'd hidden it in her pocket. Instead, he touched her elbow and Serena turned to him. *This was his chance.* Dan wished he could think of something beautiful and passionate to say, but his heart was in his mouth. Before his nerves could paralyze him, he leaned in and kissed her on the lips, ever so gently. The earth wobbled on its axis. He was glad he was sitting down. When he pulled back, Serena's eyes were glowing at him.

She wiped her nose with the back of her hand and smiled at him. Then she lifted her chin and kissed Dan again. Just a tiny kiss on his lower lip, before she ducked her head down and leaned it against his shoulder. Dan closed his eyes to steady himself.

Oh God. What is she thinking? he wondered desperately. *Why won't she tell me?*

"So where do Westsiders go to hang out?" Serena asked. "Is there a place like this?"

"Not really," Dan said, his arm around her. He didn't want to have a conversation right now. He wanted to take her hand and dive off the edge of the cliff and float on their backs in a moonlit sea. He wanted to kiss her again. And again and again. "I go down to the boat basin during the day, sometimes. At night we just walk around."

20

"The boat basin," Serena repeated. "Will you take me there?"
Dan nodded. He'd take her anywhere.

He waited for Serena to lift her head so they could kiss again. But Serena kept her head pressed into his shoulder, breathing in the smoky scent of Dan's coat and allowing her nerves be soothed.

They sat like that for a little while longer. Dan was too nervous and happy and dazed to even light a cigarette. He was hoping they could fall asleep that way and wake up in the pink light of dawn, still wrapped in each other's arms.

A few minutes later, Serena pulled away. "I'd better go before I fall asleep," she said, standing up. She leaned down and kissed Dan on the cheek. Her hair brushed his ear and he shivered. "See you soon, okay?"

Dan nodded. *Do you have to go?* He was afraid to open his mouth in case he said the words that had been threatening to escape all night. *I love you.* He was still so afraid of scaring her away.

He watched Serena run across the street, her pale hair streaming out behind her. The doorman held the door to her building open, and she disappeared.

Serena rode up in the elevator, jangling her keys in her coat pocket. A few weeks ago she would have been sitting at home on a Friday night, watching TV and feeling sorry for herself. How lucky she was to have made a new friend in Dan.

Dan sat on the Met steps for a few more minutes until the lights came on in the top floor of the building across the street. He imagined Serena kicking off her boots in the hall and dropping her coat in a chair for the maid to pick up. She'd change into a long, white silk nightgown and sit in front of a gilt-framed mirror, brushing her long, golden hair, like a princess in a fairy tale. Dan touched his lower lip with his index finger. Had he really kissed her? He'd done it so many times in his dreams it was almost impossible to believe that it had actually happened.

He stood up, rubbed his eyes, and stretched his arms up high above his head. God, he felt good. It was funny—all of a sudden, he was the guy he usually hated reading about in books. The happiest guy alive.

strike two!

"I don't see why you have to go to Brown on the same weekend that I'm going to Yale," Blair called out to Nate from inside her bathroom. Nate was lying on her bed in the adjoining room, snaking one of Blair's belts around on top of the bedspread for Kitty Minky, Blair's Russian Blue cat, to chase. The lights were out, the candles were lit, Macy Gray was playing on the stereo, and Nate had his shirt off.

"Nate?" Blair repeated impatiently. She began to take off her clothes and pile them on the bathroom floor. Her plan had been for them to go up to New Haven together that weekend. They could rent a car and stay at a romantic bed-and-breakfast, as if they were on their honeymoon.

"Yeah," Nate finally answered. "I don't know. That's just when Brown scheduled my interview. Sorry." He snapped the belt from between Kitty Minky's paws and cracked it in the air above her head, sending her streaking into the closet. Then he rolled over onto his back and stared up at the ceiling, waiting.

The last time he and Blair had been about to have sex, Nate had spilled the beans about doing it with Serena the summer before she'd gone away to boarding school. It had just seemed too slimy to go through with it without Blair knowing that A) it wasn't his first time and B) he'd done it with her former best friend. Of course, once he'd confessed, Blair hadn't wanted to do it anymore. She'd been furious.

Thankfully, all that was behind them. Well, sort of.

Blair finished strapping on the Manolos and spritzed herself with perfume. She closed her eyes and counted to three. *One, two, three.* In those three seconds she played a short film in her head, imagining the incredible night she and Nate were about to have. They were childhood lovers, destined to be together, giving themselves wholly to one another. She opened her eyes and ran the brush through her hair one more time, checking out her reflection in the mirror. She looked confident and ready. She looked like someone who always got what she wanted. She was the girl who was going to get into Yale and marry the boy. If only her nostrils weren't quite so big or her breasts so small, but whatever.

She pushed open the bathroom door.

Nate looked up and was surprised to find himself immediately turned on. Maybe it was the champagne or the steak. He closed his eyes and opened them again. No, Blair really did look that good. He reached for her hand and pulled her down on top of him. They kissed, their lips and tongues playing the same games with each other that they'd been playing for two years. But this time the game wasn't going to be like some four-hour session of Monopoly that the players eventually got sick of and abandoned. This game was going somewhere, and they weren't going to stop until they had bought up every piece of real estate they could lay their hands on.

Blair closed her eyes and pretended she was Audrey Hepburn in *Love in the Afternoon*. She loved old movies, particularly ones with Audrey Hepburn in them. They never showed the characters having sex in those movies. The love scenes were always romantic and tasteful, with lots of long, heartfelt kisses, great outfits, and cool hairdos. Blair tried to keep her shoulders down and her neck stretched long so she would feel tall and lean and sensuous in Nate's arms.

Nate accidentally jabbed her in the ribs with his elbow. "Ow," Blair said, pulling away. She hadn't meant to sound scared when she said it, but she was, a little. Audrey Hepburn never got jabbed in the ribs by Cary Grant, not even accidentally. He treated her like a china doll.

"Sorry," mumbled Nate. "Here." He reached for a pillow and slid it under her so that her head and shoulders were propped up comfortably. Blair lifted her head and fanned her hair out prettily around her face. Then she reached up and bit Nate on the shoulder, leaving an *o* of white teeth marks on his skin.

"There, that's what you get for hurting me," she said, batting her eyelashes.

"I promise to be careful," said Nate seriously, sliding his hand over her hip and down her leg.

Blair took a deep breath and tried to relax her whole body. This wasn't like any of the love scenes in any of her favorite old movies. She hadn't thought it would feel this real or be quite so awkward.

Nothing ever *looks* as good as it does in the movies, but it should still feel nice.

Nate kissed Blair softly, and she touched the back of his neck and smelled his familiar Nate smell. Bravely, she reached down with her other hand and tried to unbuckle his belt.

"It's stuck," she said, plucking at the confusing tangle of leather and metal. Her cheeks flamed uncomfortably. She'd never felt so uncoordinated.

"I'll do it," Nate offered. He quickly undid the buckle as Blair cast her gaze around her room, her eyes settling on an old oil painting of her grandmother as a young girl, holding a basket of rose petals. Blair suddenly felt very naked.

She turned back to Nate, watching as he pulled his pants down, kicking them off over his ankles and feet. The crotch of his red-and-white checked boxers stuck out, tentlike.

She sucked in her breath.

Then the front door to the apartment creaked open and slammed loudly shut.

"Hello? Anyone home?"

It was Blair's mother.

Blair and Nate both froze. Her mother and Cyrus, her mother's new boyfriend, had gone to the opera. They weren't supposed to be home for hours.

"Blair darling? Are you here? Cyrus and I have something exciting to tell you!"

"Blair?" Cyrus's loud voice reverberated against the walls.

Blair pushed Nate off of her and pulled the comforter up to her neck.

"What should we do?" Nate whispered. He slid his hand under the comforter and touched Blair's stomach.

Bad move. *Never* touch a girl's stomach unless she asks you to. It makes her feel fat.

Blair shrank away from him and rolled over, dropping her feet to the floor.

"Blair?" Her mother's voice was just outside the bedroom door. "Can I come in for a moment? It's important."

Whoa.

"Hold on!" Blair shouted. She lunged for her closet and whipped out a pair of sweatpants. "Get dressed," she hissed at Nate. She kicked off her Manolos and scrambled into her sweatpants and her father's old Yale sweatshirt. Nate pulled his pants back on and redid his belt buckle. Strike two on the sex thing.

"Ready?" Blair whispered.

Disappointed, Nate nodded silently in response.

Blair pushed open her bedroom door to find her mother waiting for her in the hallway. Eleanor Waldorf beamed happily at her daughter, her cheeks flushed with red wine and excitement.

"Notice anything different?" she asked, waggling the fingers of her left hand in the air. On her ring finger flashed an enormous diamond set in gold. It looked like a traditional engagement ring, just four times the usual size. It was ridiculous.

Blair stared at it, frozen in the doorway to her bedroom. She could feel Nate's breath on her ear from where he stood behind her. Neither of them said anything.

"Cyrus asked me to marry him!" her mother exclaimed. "Isn't that wonderful?"

Blair stared at her in disbelief.

Cyrus Rose was balding and had a small, bristly mustache. He wore a gold bracelet and ugly, double-breasted pinstriped suits. Her mother had met him last spring in the cosmetics department at Saks. He was shopping for perfume for his mother and Eleanor had offered to help him. She came home reeking of the stuff, Blair remembered. "I even gave him my number," her mother had said with a giggle, making Blair want to puke. Much to Blair's disgust and dismay, Cyrus had called and kept calling. And now they were getting married.

Just then, Cyrus Rose appeared at the end of the hall. "Whaddya think, Blair?" he asked, winking at her. He was wearing a blue double-breasted suit and shiny black shoes. His face was red. His stomach stuck out. His eyes bulged out of his head like those of a blowfish. He rubbed together his fat, stubby hands with their hairy wrists and cheesy gold jewelry.

Her new stepfather. Blair's stomach churned queasily. So much for losing her virginity to the boy she loved. The movie of her actual life was turning out to be much more tragic and much more absurd.

Blair pursed her lips and gave her mother a small, stiff peck on the cheek. "Congratulations, Mom," she said.

"Thatta girl," boomed Cyrus.

"Congratulations, Mrs. Waldorf," said Nate, stepping around Blair.

He felt awkward participating in such an intimate family moment. Couldn't Blair have just told her mom to wait and talked to her in the morning?

Mrs. Waldorf kept hugging him. "Isn't life wonderful?" she said.

Nate wasn't so sure.

Blair sighed resignedly and padded down the hall in her bare feet to congratulate Cyrus. He smelled like bleu cheese and sweat. He had hair growing out of the top of his nose. He was going to be her new stepdad. She still refused to believe it.

"I'm happy for you, Cyrus," Blair said stiffly. She stood on tiptoe and put her smooth, cool cheek near his hot, whiskery mouth.

"We're the luckiest people in the world," Cyrus said, giving her a revolting wet kiss on the cheek.

Blair didn't feel very lucky.

Eleanor released Nate. "The best part is we're doing it fast," she said. Blair turned to her mother and blinked. "We're getting married the Saturday after Thanksgiving," her mother continued. "That's only three weeks away!"

Blair stopped blinking. The Saturday after Thanksgiving? But that was her birthday. Her seventeenth.

"It's going to be at the St. Claire. And I want lots of bridesmaids. My sisters and your friends. Of course, you'll be the maid of honor. You can help me plan. It's going to be so much fun, Blair," her mother said breathlessly. "I just love weddings!"

"Okay," Blair responded, her voice completely devoid of emotion. "Should I tell Dad?"

Her mother paused, remembering. "How's your father?" she asked, still beaming. Nothing was going to put a damper on her bliss.

"Great." Blair shrugged. "He got me a pair of shoes. And a really nice cake."

"Cake?" Cyrus asked eagerly.

Pig, Blair thought. At least her father had given her a birthday, because it didn't look like her real one was going to be much fun. "Sorry we didn't bring any home," she said. "I forgot."

Eleanor ran her hands over her hips. "Well, I can't eat any anyway. The bride has to watch her figure!" She glanced at Cyrus and giggled.

"Mom?" Blair said.

"Yes, sweetheart?"

"Do you mind if Nate and I go back in my room and watch some TV?" Blair asked.

"Of course not. You go right ahead," her mother said, smiling knowingly at Nate.

Cyrus winked at them. "Nighty-night, Blair," he said. "Night, Nate."

"Good night, Mr. Rose," Nate said and followed Blair back into her bedroom.

The minute Nate shut the door, Blair threw herself onto her bed facedown, her head buried in her arms.

"Come on, Blair," Nate said, sitting down at the end of the bed and rubbing her feet. "Cyrus is okay. I mean, it could be worse, right? He could be a total asshole."

"He *is* a total asshole," Blair murmured. "I hate him." All of a sudden she wished Nate would just leave her alone to suffer. He couldn't understand; no one could.

Nate lay down beside her and stroked her hair.

"Am *I* a total asshole?" he asked.

"No."

"Do you hate me?"

"No," Blair said into the comforter.

"Come here," Nate said, tugging on her arm.

He pulled her toward him and slid his hands beneath her sweatshirt, hoping they'd get back to where they'd left off. He kissed her neck.

Blair closed her eyes and tried to relax. She could do this. She could go ahead and have sex and millions of orgasms even though her mother and Cyrus were in the next room. She could.

Except she couldn't. Blair wanted her first time to be perfect, and this was anything but. Her mom and Cyrus were probably fooling around in her mom's bedroom right now. Just thinking about it made her feel like her skin was crawling with lice or something.

This was all wrong. Everything was wrong. Her life was a complete disaster.

Blair pulled away from Nate and buried her face in a pillow. "I'm sorry," she said, although she didn't feel very sorry. This was no time for the pleasures of the flesh. She felt like Joan of Arc as played by Ingrid Bergman in the original movie—a beautiful, untouchable martyr.

Nate went back to stroking her hair and rubbing the small of her back, hoping she'd change her mind. But Blair kept her face stubbornly pressed into the pillow. He couldn't help wondering if she'd ever really intended to do it with him.

After a few minutes he stopped rubbing her back and stood up. It was late, and he was getting tired and bored.

"I have to get home," he said.

Blair pretended not to hear him. She was too caught up in the drama of her own misery.

"Call me," Nate said.

And then he left.

s is determined to stay lucky

On Saturday morning, Serena woke to the sound of her mother's voice.

"Serena? Can I come in?"

"What?" said Serena, sitting up in bed. She still wasn't used to living with her parents again. It kind of sucked.

The door opened a few inches. "I have some news for you," her mother told her.

Serena didn't really mind that her mother had woken her up, but she didn't want her mother to think she could just barge into her room uninvited any time she felt like it. "Okay," she said, sounding more annoyed than she really felt.

Mrs. van der Woodsen came in and sat down on the end of the bed. She was wearing a navy blue silk dressing gown by Oscar de la Renta and matching navy blue silk slippers. Her wavy blond-highlighted hair was pulled up in a loose bun on top of her head, and her pale skin had a pearly sheen from years of using La Mer skin cream. She smelled like Chanel No. 5.

Serena pulled her knees up under her chin and covered her legs with the comforter. "What's up?" she said.

"Eleanor Waldorf just called a minute ago," her mother told her. "And guess what?"

Serena rolled her eyes at her mother's attempt at suspense. "What?"

"She's getting married."

"To that Cyrus guy?"

"Yes, of course. Who else would she marry?" her mother said, brushing imaginary crumbs from her dressing gown.

"I don't know," Serena said. She frowned, wondering how Blair had taken the news. Probably not very well. Even though Blair hadn't been very nice to Serena lately, Serena could still empathize with her old friend.

"The unusual thing is," continued Mrs. van der Woodsen, "they're doing it just like that." She snapped her bejeweled fingers.

"What do you mean?" Serena said.

"Thanksgiving weekend," her mother whispered and raised her eyebrows to make the point that this was very unusual indeed. "The Saturday after Thanksgiving. That's the wedding date. And she wants you to be a bridesmaid. I'm sure Blair will fill you in on all the details. She's the maid of honor."

Mrs. Waldorf stood up and began straightening the scattered Creed perfume bottles, little boxes of Tiffany jewelry, and tubes of Stila makeup on top of Serena's dresser.

"Don't do that, Mom," Serena whined and closed her eyes.

The Saturday after Thanksgiving. That was only three weeks away. It was also Blair's birthday, Serena realized. Poor Blair. She loved her birthday. It was *her* day. Obviously not this year, though.

And what was it going to be like to be a bridesmaid when Blair was the maid of honor? Would Blair purposely make her wear a dress that didn't fit? Would she spike her champagne?

Make her walk down the aisle with Chuck Bass, the slimiest boy in their old circle of friends? It was too weird to even imagine.

Her mother sat down on the bed again and stroked Serena's hair. "What's wrong, darling?" she asked, worriedly. "I thought you'd be excited about being a bridesmaid."

Serena opened her eyes. "I have a headache, that's all," she sighed, pulling the comforter around her. "I think I'm going to just lie here and watch TV for a while, okay?"

Her mother patted her foot. "All right. I'll send Deidre in with some coffee and juice for you. I think she bought some croissants, too."

"Thanks, Mom," Serena said.

Her mother stood up and went to the door. She paused and turned around to smile brilliantly at her daughter. "Autumn weddings are always so lovely. I think this is quite exciting."

"Yes," Serena said, fluffing up her pillow. "It's going to be great."

Her mother left, and Serena rolled over and stared out her window for a minute, watching birds take flight from the bronzed treetops surrounding the roof of the Met. Then she reached for the phone and pressed the speed-dial button for her brother Erik's number at Brown. Whenever she needed reassurance, it was the first button she pressed. With her other hand she clicked the power button on her TV's remote. *SpongeBob SquarePants* was on Nickelodeon. She stared at it without really seeing it, listening as the phone rang three times, then four.

On the sixth ring, Erik answered. "Yeah?"

"Hey," Serena said. "What are you doing up?"

"I'm not up," Erik said. He coughed loudly. "Oh, man."

Serena grinned. "Sorry. Hard night, huh?"

Erik moaned in response.

"So, the reason I'm calling is I just found out that Blair's mom is getting married to this guy, Cyrus. I don't even think they've known each other all that long, but whatever. Anyway, I have to be a bridesmaid, and Blair is the maid of honor, which means . . . I don't know what it means. But I'm pretty sure it's going to stink."

She waited for Erik to answer. "I guess you're too hungover to talk about this now, huh?" she said when he didn't.

"Kind of," Erik said.

"Okay, fine. I'll call you later," Serena said, disappointed. "Hey, I was also thinking about visiting you up there sometime soon. Like maybe next weekend?"

"Okay," Erik yawned.

"Okay. Bye," Serena said and hung up.

She rolled out from under the covers, stood up, and shuffled into the bathroom, where she examined herself in the mirror. Her gray boxer shorts were sagging in the butt, and her Mr. Bubble T-shirt was twisted around and hanging off one shoulder. Her straight blond hair was plastered to the back of her neck, and a thin line of crusted drool had dried on one cheek.

Of course, she still looked hot.

"Fatso," Serena said to her reflection. She reached for her toothbrush and began to brush her teeth slowly, thinking about Erik. Even though he seemed to party even harder than she did, he'd managed not to get kicked out of boarding school and had gotten into Brown. Erik was the good son, while Serena was the bad daughter. It was so unfair.

She furrowed her eyebrows determinedly as she scrubbed at her molars.

So what if she'd been kicked out of boarding school, her grades were only mediocre, and her only extracurricular was this weird movie she had made for the Constance Billard School senior film festival? She was going to show everyone that she wasn't as bad as they thought. She was going to show them by getting into a good college like Brown and becoming someone.

Not that she wasn't already someone. Serena was the girl everyone remembered. The one everyone loved to hate. She didn't have to try to shine: she shined brighter than the rest of them already.

She spat a wad of toothpaste into the sink.

Yes, she was definitely heading up to Brown next weekend, even if it was a long shot. She might get lucky. She usually did.

one lucky westsider, one lonely one

"Freak," Jenny Humphrey whispered to her reflection.

She stood in front of the mirror holding her breath and pushing her stomach out as far as it would go. It still didn't stick out as far as her boobs, which were enormous for a ninth-grader. Her pink nightgown fell in a tentlike triangle from her breasts to her knees, hiding her protruding stomach and her short little legs. She had grown *out* instead of *up* like Serena van der Woodsen, the senior at Constance Billard whom Jenny idolized. Jenny's boobs erased any hope of her ever looking remotely cool, like Serena. They were the bane of her existence.

Jenny let out her breath and pulled her nightgown over her head so she could try on the new black tube top she'd bought at Urban Outfitters after school yesterday. She yanked it over her shoulders and down over her boobs and looked at her reflection. No longer did she have two gigantic boobs but one monster slug of a uniboob. She looked deformed.

Pushing her dark brown curly hair behind her ears, Jenny turned away from the mirror, disgusted. She pulled on a pair of old Constance Billard sweatpants and headed out to the kitchen for some tea. Her older brother, Dan, was just coming out of his room. He always looked scary in the morning, his hair wild and his eyes bleary. But this morning his eyes were huge and bright, as if he'd been up all night drinking coffee.

"So?" Jenny said as they filed into the kitchen.

She watched as Dan spooned some instant coffee grounds into a mug and ran the hot tap water over them. He wasn't particularly discerning when it came to coffee. He stood by the sink silently stirring the stuff with a spoon, watching the brown froth spin round and round.

"I know you went out with Serena last night," Jenny said, crossing her arms impatiently. "So what happened? Was it amazing? What'd she wear? What'd you do? What'd she say?"

Dan took a sip of his coffee. Jenny always got a little overexcited when it came to Serena. He enjoyed teasing her.

"Oh, come on, tell me something. What'd you guys do?" Jenny insisted.

Dan shrugged. "We ate ice cream."

Jenny put her hands on her hips. "Wow. Hot date."

Dan just smiled. He didn't care if it drove his sister nuts; he wasn't going to let go of any piece of last night. It was too precious, especially the kissing part. In fact, he'd just written a poem about it so he could relish it forever. He'd called the poem "Sweet."

"So what else? What did you do? What did she say?" Jenny prodded.

Dan filled his mug with more hot water. "I don't know—," he started to say. Then the phone rang.

Both Dan and Jenny leapt to get it. But Dan was faster.

"Hey Dan, it's Serena."

Dan pressed the phone close to his ear and walked out of the kitchen and over to the window seat in the den. Through the dust-covered pane he could see kids Rollerblading in Riverside Park and the bright autumn sun sparkling on the Hudson River beyond. Dan took a deep, calming breath. "Hey," he said.

"Listen," Serena said. "I know this is kind of a weird thing to ask, but I have to be a bridesmaid in this big wedding in three weeks, and I was wondering if you'd like to come with me, you know, as my date."

"Sure," Dan said, before she could say more.

"It's Blair Waldorf's mother's wedding," Serena said. "You know, the girl I used to be friends with?"

"Sure," Dan said again. It sounded like Serena not only wanted him to go with her, she *needed* him to go, for moral support. It made Dan feel important, and it gave him courage. He lowered his voice to a barely audible whisper, just in case Jenny was listening in the other room. "I'd really like to go up to Brown with you, too," he said. "If that's okay."

"Sure." Serena paused. "Um, I think I'm going up this Friday after school. We have half-days on Friday. Do you?"

It kind of sounded like she'd forgotten about asking Dan to come with her. But Dan decided he was hearing her wrong.

"I get out of school at two on Fridays," he told her.

"Okay, so you could meet me at Grand Central. I'm going to get the train up to our country house in Ridgefield and pick up the caretaker's car there," she said.

"Sounds good," Dan said.

"It'll be great," said Serena, sounding a bit more enthusiastic. "So thanks for agreeing to come to the wedding with me. It might be fun."

"I hope so," Dan said. He didn't see how he could not have fun with her. But he'd have to find something decent to wear. He should have kept that Barneys tux after all.

"Um, I'd better go. The maid is yelling for me to come eat my breakfast," Serena said. "So I'll call you later on, and we can make plans for next weekend, okay?"

"Okay," he said.

"'Bye."

"'Bye," said Dan. He hung up before he could say something else. *I love you.*

"That was her, right?" Jenny asked, when he returned to the kitchen.

Dan shrugged.

"What'd she say?"

"Nothing."

"Yeah, right. You were whispering," Jenny accused.

Dan pulled a bagel out of a paper bag on the kitchen counter and examined it. Surprise, surprise, it was moldy. Their dad wasn't the best housekeeper in the world. It was hard to remember to shop for groceries or mop the floors when you were busy writing essays on why some poet no one had ever heard of was the next Allen Ginsberg. Most of the time Dan and Jenny survived on Chinese takeout.

Dan threw out the bag of moldy bagels and found an unopened bag of potato chips in the cupboard. He ripped open the bag and shoved a handful of chips into his mouth. They were better than nothing.

Jenny made a face at him. "Do you have to be such an annoying idiot?" she said. "I already know it was Serena on the phone. Why can't you just tell me what she said?"

"She wants me to go to a wedding with her. That Blair

girl's mother is getting married, and Serena is going to be a bridesmaid. She wants me there with her," Dan explained.

"You're going to Mrs. Waldorf's wedding?" Jenny gasped. "Where is it?"

Dan shrugged. "I don't know, I didn't ask," he said.

Jenny bristled. "I can't believe this. It's like, all this time you and Dad were so totally against all those fancy girls I go to school with and their ritzy families. And now you're like, going out with the queen of all of them and getting invited to incredible weddings. It's so unfair!"

Dan shoved another handful of potato chips in his mouth. "Sorry," he said with his mouth full.

"Well, I just hope you haven't forgotten that I was the one who like, told you that you even had a chance with Serena," Jenny huffed. She flung her used teabag angrily into the sink. "Do you realize that wedding's probably going to be in like, *Vogue?* I can't believe you're going."

But Dan was barely listening. In his mind he was riding on a train, holding hands with Serena and gazing into the deep blue depths of her eyes.

"Did she say anything about tomorrow?" Jenny asked him.

Dan stared at her blankly.

"Me and Vanessa and Serena are supposed to meet at Vanessa's boyfriend's bar in Williamsburg to go over the film we helped Serena make for the Constance film festival. Make sure it's all set to go."

Another blank look.

"I thought maybe she would have invited you."

No response.

Jenny sighed, exasperated. Dan was hopeless, she realized, so entirely lovesick that she might as well forget about trying to get any information out of him. He hadn't even asked why she was wearing a black tube top around the house on a Saturday morning. Suddenly Jenny felt extremely lonely. She had always relied on her brother for company, but now he was flaking out on her.

She definitely needed to find some other friends.

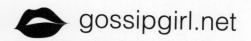

gossipgirl.net

Disclaimer: All the real names of places, people, and events have been altered or abbreviated to protect the innocent. Namely, me.

hey people!

THE WEDDING OF THE YEAR

This time of year is usually a little dull, with nothing much happening until the holiday party season. But **B**'s mother has given us all something to talk about. I mean, how long have she and her boyfriend known each other, anyway? Like two or three months? If I were going to spend the rest of my life with someone, or even a weekend, I'd want to know them better than that. Anyway, I've heard he is seriously tacky, so the wedding is definitely going to be a sight to behold. And how is **B** going to have any fun when she has **S** to deal with?? I smell a catfight, and it's not going to be pretty. Yay! I can't wait!

Your E-Mail

Hey GG,
I don't know if you knew this already, but **B**'s gonna have a new stepbro. I'm in his class at school, and he's kind of out there. But he's also pretty cute. ;)
—BronxKat

Dear BronxKat,
All I can say is this whole wedding thing is looking better and better!
—GG

i heard **b**'s dad gave yale like a million dollars so she doesn't even have to try very hard to get in. anyways i bet **n** and **b** aren't going to wind up at the same college next year. what do you think?
—bookwrm

Dear bookwrm,
I'm not making any bets yet. *B* is more unpredictable than she seems. . . .
—GG

SPEAKING OF COLLEGE . . .

Now's the time when we're all supposed to be freaking out, looking at all the pictures in the college catalogs we've sent for, imagining ourselves talking to hot boys on green lawns in front of massive, ivy-clad, brick buildings. Now's the time when we're supposed to look back at all those tests we blew off or volunteer work we didn't do and kick ourselves for being so stupid and lazy. Now's the time when the goody-goodies are applying early-decision and making us normal people feel like crap. Well, I refuse to let it get me down. Here's my recipe for senior stress management: Mix one gorgeous boy with a nice new pair of leather boots, a new cashmere sweater, a long night out, and several drinks. Stir in a very late morning and hot chocolate in bed. Begin working on your college applications when you're good and ready. See? There's no need to get all stressed out.

Sightings

N at **Asphalt Green,** playing tennis with his dad. *B* at the cinema on Eighty-sixth, watching some action flick with her little brother. Guess she'd rather watch guys shooting at each other from burning helicopters than hang out at home with Mom, discussing dresses and cakes and caterers. *S* buying perfume at **Barneys.** I swear, that girl is in there practically every day. *D* scribbling in a notebook down by the Seventy-ninth Street Boat Basin. Another love poem about *S* perhaps? *J* returning a black tube top at **Urban Outfitters.**

More soon!

You know you love me,

b is determined to make n want her

"Come and have pancakes, darling," Mrs. Waldorf called down the hall, hoping to unearth Blair from her room. "I had Myrtle make them nice and thin, just the way you like them."

Blair opened her bedroom door and stuck her head out. "Hold on," she said. "I'm getting dressed."

"There's no need, dear. Cyrus and I are still in our jammies," Blair's mother said perkily. She retied the cord on her green silk dressing gown. Cyrus was wearing one just like it. They'd bought them yesterday at Saks after sizing wedding rings at Cartier. Then they'd gone to the dark and cozy King Cole bar in the St. Regis Hotel to drink champagne. Cyrus had even joked about getting a room. It was so romantic.

Gross.

"Just hold on," Blair repeated stubbornly, and her mother retreated to the dining room. Blair sat on the edge of her bed, looking at her reflection in the closet mirror. She'd lied to her mother just then. In truth, she'd been up for hours and was already completely dressed in jeans, a black turtleneck, and boots. She'd even painted her nails dark brown to suit her mood.

Mirror, mirror, on the wall, who's the fairest of them all? Not Blair—at least not today.

She'd spent her entire Saturday feeling pissed off. Then she'd gone to bed pissed off, and she'd woken up pissed off on Sunday morning. In fact, it looked like she was going to spend the rest of her life permanently pissed off. Nate hadn't tried to see her since Friday night, so he was obviously more than a little disappointed about what had happened. She was still a virgin. Her mother was marrying an obnoxious idiot. And the date they'd chosen for their wedding happened to be Blair's most important birthday ever.

Oh, yes, her life definitely sucked, big-time.

Since it couldn't suck any worse than it already did, and because she was hungry, Blair got up and headed out to the dining room to eat pancakes with her mother and Cyrus.

"There she is," Cyrus boomed loudly. He patted the seat next to him. "Come, sit."

Blair did as she was told. She picked up the platter laden with pancakes and forked a few onto her plate.

"Don't take the one with the hole in the middle," her eleven-year-old brother, Tyler, told her. "It's mine." Tyler was wearing a Led Zeppelin T-shirt and had a red bandanna tied around his head. He wanted to be a rock-and-roll journalist and modeled himself after Cameron Crowe, the movie director who'd toured with Led Zeppelin when he was only like fifteen. Tyler had a huge collection of vinyl and kept an antique hookah pipe under his bed. Not that he'd ever used it. Blair was concerned that Tyler was turning into a freak who was going to have trouble making friends. Her parents thought it was cute, as long as he wore his Brooks Brothers suit to St. George's every morning like a good boy and got into a good boarding school.

In the world Blair and her friends lived in, everyone's parents were like that—as long as their kids didn't screw up and embarrass them, they could basically do whatever they wanted. In fact, that was the mistake Serena had made. She'd been caught screwing up, and getting caught was unacceptable. She ought to have known better.

Blair poured maple syrup over her pancakes and then rolled each of them up like a burrito, just the way she liked them.

Her mother snagged a grape from the fruit bowl and popped it into Cyrus's mouth. He hummed happily as he chewed and swallowed it. Then he puckered up his lips like a fish, begging for more. Mrs. Waldorf giggled and fed him another one. Blair rolled her pancake burritos around in their syrup, ignoring their revolting display.

"I've been on the phone with the man at the St. Claire all morning," her mother told her. "He's very flamboyant and very concerned about the décor. He's hilarious."

"Flamboyant? You mean gay. It's okay to say 'gay,' Mom," Blair said.

"Yes, well . . . ," her mother stuttered uncomfortably. She didn't like to say the word *gay*. Not after having been married to one—it was too humiliating.

"We're trying to decide if we should book a few suites in the hotel," Cyrus said. "You girls could use one for changing into your gowns and doing your hair. And who knows—some of our guests might get so tipsy they'll want to crash out until morning." He laughed and winked at Blair's mother.

Suites?

Suddenly Blair had an idea. She and Nate could get a suite! What more perfect place and time to lose your virginity than in a suite at the St. Claire on your seventeenth birthday?

Blair put her fork down, dabbed gently at the corners of her mouth with her napkin, and smiled sweetly at her mother. "Can you book a suite for me and my friends?" she asked.

"Of course we can," Eleanor said. "That's a fine idea."

"Thanks, Mom," Blair said, smiling excitedly into her coffee cup. She couldn't wait to tell Nate.

"There's so much to do," her mother said anxiously. "I've been making lists in my sleep."

Cyrus took her hand and kissed it. The diamond blazed on her finger. "Don't worry, Bunny," Cyrus said, as if he were talking to a two-year-old.

Blair picked up a dripping pancake roll in her fingers and shoved it in her mouth.

"Of course I want your input on everything, Blair," her mother told her. "You have such good taste."

Blair shrugged and chewed, her cheeks bulging.

"And we can't wait for you to meet Aaron," Eleanor said.

Blair stopped chewing. "Who's Aaron?" she said with her mouth full.

"My son, Aaron?" Cyrus said. "You knew I had a son, didn't you, Blair?"

Blair shook her head. She didn't know anything about Cyrus. He might as well have wandered in off the street and asked her mother to marry him. The less she knew about him the better.

"He's a senior at Bronxdale Prep. Smart kid. Skipped tenth grade. He's only sixteen, a graduating senior, college bound!" Cyrus announced proudly.

"Isn't that impressive?" Blair's mother chimed in. "And he's so good-looking too."

"That he is," Cyrus agreed. "He'll knock your socks off."

Blair reached for another pancake from the platter. She didn't care to listen to Cyrus and her mother go on and on about some geek wearing a pocket protector who skipped grades for fun. She could imagine Aaron exactly: a skinny version of Cyrus, with zits and greasy hair and braces and horrible clothes. The apple of his father's eye.

"Hey, that's mine!" Tyler whined, dinging Blair's fork with his knife. "Hand it over."

Blair could see now that the pancake she'd taken had a finger-sized hole in the middle of it. "Sorry," she said and passed her plate across the table to Tyler. "Take it."

"So, will you stay home today and help me?" her mother asked. "I've got a whole stack of wedding books and magazines for us to go through."

Blair pushed her chair back abruptly. She couldn't think of a worse way to spend the day. "Sorry," she said. "I've already made plans."

It was a lie, but Blair was sure that as soon as she was finished talking to Nate, she would indeed have plans. They could see a movie, go for a walk in the park, hang out at his place, plan their night at the St. Claire. . . .

Wrong.

"Sorry, I'm meeting Anthony and the guys in the park to play ball," Nate said. "I told you that yesterday."

"No, you didn't. Yesterday you said you had to hang out with your dad. You said maybe we could do something today," Blair complained. "I never get to see you."

"Well, I'm heading over there now," Nate said. "Sorry."

"But I wanted to tell you something," she said, trying to sound mysterious.

"What?"

"I'd really rather tell you in person."

"Come on, Blair," Nate said impatiently. "I have to go."

"Okay. Fine. What I wanted to tell you was that my mom and Cyrus are getting suites at the St. Claire for their wedding.

And seeing how it's going to be my birthday and everything, I thought that maybe that would be the perfect time for us to . . . you know . . . *do it*."

Nate was silent.

"Nate?" Blair asked.

"Yeah?"

"So what do you think?"

"I don't know," he said. "It sounds fine. Look, I have to get going, okay?"

Blair clutched the phone to her ear. "Nate?" she said. "Do you still love me?"

But Nate was already hanging up. "I'll call you later, okay?" he said. " 'Bye."

Blair clicked off and stared at the Persian rug on the floor of her bedroom, the pancakes churning uncomfortably in her stomach. But before she could even think about sticking her finger down her throat, she had to come up with a plan.

She wasn't going to see Nate today, and they probably wouldn't see each other during the week, what with her one hundred and one extracurriculars and his sports. And next weekend she was going up to Yale and he was going to Brown. She couldn't let a whole week go by with Nate mad at her for shutting him down Friday night and her worrying about him being mad at her. She had to *do* something.

If only she and Nate could have had the kind of romantic fights couples had in movies. First they would yell hurtful things at each other until she began to cry. She would grab her purse and her coat, fumbling with the buttons because she was so upset. Then, just as she was shakily opening the front door, preparing to walk out of his life forever, he would come up behind her and wrap his arms around her, holding her tight. She would turn around and look searchingly up at him for a moment, and then they would kiss passionately. In the end, he'd beg her to stay, and then they would make love.

The real thing was so much more boring, but Blair knew how to spice things up.

She imagined walking over to Nate's town house dressed in a long black coat, a silk scarf wrapped around her head, her face masked by huge Chanel sunglasses. She'd drop off a special gift for Nate, and then disappear into the night. When he opened the gift, he'd smell her perfume and long for her.

Forgetting all about making herself sick, Blair stood up and grabbed her purse, ready to hit Barneys.

But what do you get for a boy to remind him that he loves you and wants you more than ever?

Hmm. That's a hard one. . . .

to catch a thief

"So tell me why you're calling me again?" Erik said grumpily.

"Nice to talk to you, too," Serena joked. "I'm just calling to tell you that I'm definitely coming up to Brown next weekend. I have an interview scheduled for Saturday at twelve."

"Okay," Erik said. "We usually have a party on Saturday nights. Hope you don't mind."

"Mind?" Serena laughed. "That's perfect. Oh, and I'm probably bringing a friend."

"What kind of friend?" Erik said.

"Just this guy Dan I've been hanging out with. You'll like him, I promise," she said.

"Cool," Erik said. "Listen, I'm kind of busy. I have to go."

Serena realized that Erik was most likely not alone. He always had at least three girlfriends whom he slept with on a rotating basis.

"You're such a stud. Okay. See you soon," Serena said and clicked off. She stood up, padded over to her closet, and opened the door to get dressed.

Inside were all the same boring clothes she always wore. But she was going to college next year, maybe even to Brown. Didn't she deserve to buy herself something new?

She pulled on a worn pair of Diesel jeans and a black cashmere sweater, getting ready to go to her favorite place in the whole wide world: Barneys.

When she got there, Barneys was already crowded with Upper East Siders who had wandered in, unable to resist. The buzzing, brightly lit ground floor, its glass cases filled with unique jewelry, gorgeous gloves, and one-of-a-kind purses, and its countertops littered with sleek beauty products, made every day feel like Christmas. At the Creed counter, Serena admired the pretty glass perfume bottles with the same delight as a small child in a toy store. Moving on to the Kiehl's counter, she was tempted by a jar of deep-cleansing natural clay face masque. Of course, she already had enough beauty products to last ten years, but she loved trying out new ones. It was kind of an addiction.

Nothing wrong with that. There are definitely worse addictions.

Serena was about to ask the man behind the counter if the masque was okay to use on her skin, which tended to be dry, when she noticed a familiar figure striding purposefully through the store to the men's department.

It was Blair Waldorf. Serena put down the jar of masque and followed her.

Blair wasn't sure if Barneys was going to have what she was looking for, but that was because she didn't know what she was looking for. Nate wasn't going to be impressed by a new sweater or a nice pair of leather gloves. She had to find something unique. Sexy but not cheesy. It had to be cool. And it had to remind Nate that he still loved and wanted her. Blair headed straight for the underwear department.

First she found a table covered with an assortment of colorful cotton boxer shorts. Further on were racks of luxuriously soft terrycloth bathrobes and flannel nightshirts, shelves filled with boxes of plain old tighty-whiteys, and skeevy bikini/thong-type pants. None of these would serve. Then Blair caught sight of a rack of gray cashmere drawstring pajama bottoms.

She pulled a pair off the hanger and held them up. MADE IN ENGLAND, the tag said. PRICE: $360.00. They were casual yet sophisticated. Handsome, yet so soft and delicate that the idea of them brushing up against Nate's bare skin made Blair feel almost motherly. She crumpled the pajama bottoms in her hands and pressed them against her cheek. The scent of fine cashmere filled her nostrils and she closed her eyes, imagining Nate wearing the pajama bottoms without a shirt, his perfect chest exposed as he poured them each a glass of champagne in their St. Clair Hotel suite.

They were definitely sexy. There was no question about it: She had to have them.

Serena pretended to be very interested in a red terrycloth Ralph Lauren bathrobe, size extra large. It was big enough to shield her from Blair, and the rack it was hanging on was set up so that her view of Blair was completely unobstructed. She wondered if Blair was buying something for Nate. Probably. Lucky guy: the pajamas she was looking at were gorgeous.

Back in the good old days, Blair would have asked Serena to help her pick out a present for Nate. Not anymore.

"Are you looking for a gift for someone?" a sales guy asked, approaching Serena. He looked like a bodybuilder, bald and tan and practically busting out of his suit.

"No, I—" Serena faltered. She didn't want the man to start

dragging her around the store, showing her things, and risk being seen. "Yes. For my brother. He needs a new bathrobe."

"Is this his size?" the sales guy asked, pointing to the one she'd been looking at.

"Yes, it's perfect," Serena said. "I'll take it." Her eyes darted over to Blair, who was walking to the counter carrying the pajama bottoms. "Can I just give you my credit card here?" Serena asked the guy, turning to bat her long-lashed blue eyes at him. She pulled her credit card out of her wallet and handed it to him.

"Yes, of course," he said, whisking the bathrobe off the hanger and taking her card. "I'll be right back."

"It's a gift," Blair told the man behind the counter, handing him her credit card. The card had her name on it, but it wasn't actually *hers*. It came out of her mother's account. Blair's parents didn't give her an allowance, they just let her buy whatever she needed, within reason. A pair of nearly four-hundred-dollar pajama bottoms for Nate when it wasn't even Christmas didn't exactly fall into the "within reason" category, but Blair would find a way to convince her mother that the purchase had been absolutely necessary.

"I'm sorry, miss," the man behind the counter told her, "but your credit card has been denied." He handed the card back. "Is there another card you'd like to use?"

"*Denied?*" Blair repeated. Her face felt hot. This had never happened to her before. "Are you sure?"

"Yes. Quite sure," said the man. "Would you like to use our phone to call your bank?"

"No, that's okay," Blair said. "I'll just come back some other time." She put her credit card back in her wallet, grabbed the pajama bottoms, and turned away, heading back to the rack where she'd found them. The cashmere felt so buttery soft in her hands it made her sick to think of leaving the store without them. What was the deal, anyway? It wasn't like the money in her mother's account had just, like, *run out*. But she couldn't exactly call her mom and ask her about it, since she'd lied to get out of the house, saying she was going to a movie with Nate.

The man had removed the heavy plastic security tag, Blair noticed before she put the pajama bottoms back on the rack. She also noticed that there were lots more pairs of gray cashmere pajama bottoms left. Would they really mind if she just . . . *took them?* It wasn't like she hadn't tried to pay for them. Besides, she spent enough money in Barneys. She deserved a free gift.

Serena waited for the burly sales guy to come back with the bathrobe she hadn't meant to buy and her credit card receipt. She watched Blair start to put the pajama bottoms back and then stop.

"I'll just need your signature at the *X*," the sales guy told Serena. She turned around, and he handed her a big black Barneys shopping bag with the robe tucked neatly into a black box inside.

"Thanks," Serena said. She took the credit card slip and knelt down on the floor to sign it, using the box as a surface. Across the carpeted floor, she saw Blair crouch down between two racks of flannel nightshirts and stuff the pair of cashmere pajama bottoms hastily into her purse.

Serena couldn't believe it. Blair was stealing!

"Thanks so much," Serena said, standing up. She pressed the receipt into the sales guy's hand, grabbed her shopping bag, and headed for the exit. Even though she had done nothing wrong, seeing Blair steal made her feel like she had. She couldn't wait to get out of there. After pushing her way out onto the street, she turned up Madison, walking quickly. The shopping bag banged against her leg as she took in big gulps of crisp, autumn air. She'd gone into Barneys to look for something cool and fun for herself and had come out with a men's size extra large bathrobe. What was she doing spying on Blair, anyway? And what the hell was Blair doing stealing things? It wasn't like she was hard up or anything.

Still, Blair's secret was safe with Serena. She had no one to tell.

Blair left Barneys and turned up Madison, her pulse racing. No alarm had gone off, and no one seemed to be following her. She'd gotten away with it! Of course, she knew it was wrong to steal, especially when you had plenty of money to pay for things, but it still felt kind of exhilarating to do something so completely illegal. It was like playing the villainous femme fatale in the movie instead of the pure and steadfast girl next door. Besides, this was just a one-time thing. It wasn't like she was going to turn into a major shoplifter or anything.

Then she saw something that made her stop in her tracks. At the end of the block Serena van der Woodsen's long blond hair gleamed in the sunlight as she waited for the light to change. A large black Barneys bag was slung over her arm. And just before she began to cross the street, she turned around and looked straight at Blair.

Blair ducked her head down, pretending to be looking at her Rolex. *Shit,* she thought. *Did she see me? Did she see me taking the pajama bottoms?*

Keeping her eyes down, she opened her purse and dug around for a cigarette. When she looked up again, Serena had crossed the street and was fading into the distance.

So what if she did see me? Blair told herself. She lit a cigarette with nervous fingers. Serena could go ahead and blab to everyone in the world that she'd seen Blair Waldorf stealing from Barneys, but no one would believe her.

Right?

As she walked, Blair dipped her hand into her purse and fingered the soft cashmere pajama bottoms. She couldn't wait for Nate to put them on. The minute he did, he'd know exactly how she felt about everything, and he'd love her more than ever. Nothing Serena could say would get in the way of that.

Not so fast. Giving someone stolen goods is bad karma. It can work against you in the most surprising ways.

stood up in brooklyn

"Why are you here?" Vanessa Abrams asked Dan when Dan and Jenny arrived at The Five and Dime.

Dan shrugged. "I wanted to see how Serena's film turned out," he said, as if it was no big deal.

Yeah, right, Vanessa thought. *More like you had to come worship Serena's bony ass.*

"Serena's not here yet," she told Jenny and Dan as they looked around. The dimly lit bar was nearly empty, with only two twenty-something guys sitting at a table in the back reading the Sunday *Times* and smoking cigarettes.

"But it's one-thirty," Jenny said, looking at her watch. "We were supposed to meet at one."

Vanessa shrugged. "You know how she is."

It was true, they did know. Serena was always late. Neither Dan nor Jenny minded, though. It was an honor to be graced with her presence. But it drove Vanessa up the wall.

Clark came over and ran his fingers through Vanessa's short-cropped black hair. "You guys want something to drink?" he offered.

Vanessa grinned at him. She loved it when Clark touched her in front of Dan. It served Dan right. Clark was the bartender at The Five and Dime, the bar down the street from the apartment Vanessa shared with her older sister, Ruby. Clark was twenty-two. He had red sideburns and beautiful gray eyes, and he was the only guy she'd ever met who didn't make her feel pasty, pudgy, and odd. All this time Vanessa had thought Clark had a crush on Ruby, her cool, bass-playing, leather-pants-wearing older sister whose band played at the bar. But all along it had been Vanessa Clark was after. "You're different," he told her. "I love that."

And Vanessa *was* different. She was definitely way, way different from her classmates at the Constance Billard School for Girls. They lived with their well-to-do parents in penthouses off Fifth Avenue. She lived in a small apartment over a Spanish bodega in Williamsburg, Brooklyn. She had grown up in Vermont, but when she turned fifteen she'd begged and brooded until her artist parents had relented and let her come to New York to live with Ruby. The only condition was that she get a good, solid education at uptight Constance Billard. Vanessa's classmates didn't quite know what to make of her. While they were getting their highlights done and shopping at Barneys or Bendel's, Vanessa was shaving her own head with electric clippers and bargain hunting for logo-free jeans and T-shirts, which were always entirely black and entirely unfeminine.

Vanessa had met Dan when they'd both gotten trapped in a stairwell, locked outside of a dumb party in tenth grade, and they'd been good friends ever since. Over the past year, Vanessa and Dan had spent a lot of time together, and Vanessa had developed a terrible crush on him. But Dan had had eyes for only one girl: Serena van der Woodsen.

Vanessa was lucky Clark had found her, and she was trying to get over Dan, but it was hard. Every time she saw his scruffy, pale face and his trembling, almost birdlike hands, she felt giddy. Dan, of course, was completely oblivious. He just went on being nice to Vanessa or completely ignoring her when Serena was around, which didn't make it any easier.

Dan's sister, Jenny, worked with Vanessa on *Rancor,* Constance Billard's student-run arts magazine, for which Vanessa was editor in chief. Jenny was a talented calligrapher and photographer, with a great eye. Jenny and Vanessa had also helped Serena with her film—because she had asked, and because no one could ever say no to Serena. But Jenny had no interest in being Vanessa's friend. She was an oddball and a major fashion disaster, and not the type of girl Jenny aspired to be.

"Can you make Irish coffee?" Dan asked. It was his favorite drink because it was mostly made of coffee.

"Sure," Clark said.

"I'll just have a Coke," Jenny said. She didn't really like the taste of alcohol, except for champagne.

"So are we going to watch Serena's movie, or what?" Dan said, swiveling back and forth on his bar stool.

"We have to wait until Serena gets here, stupid," Jenny said.

Vanessa shrugged. "I'm pretty filmed out anyway," she said. "That's all I've been doing for the past three weeks."

She'd been staying up late every night to work on her film for the Constance Billard senior film festival. It was also the film she'd planned on sending to NYU along with her application. Vanessa's dream was to go to NYU next year and major in film. She wanted to be a famous director of cult masterpieces like *The Hunger* and *Ghost Dog*, but her latest effort had turned out to be kind of a disaster.

The story of her film was borrowed from a scene in Tolstoy's *War and Peace*. Dan played the lead alongside a gum-chewing Constance sophomore named Marjorie, who had no acting talent whatsoever. Vanessa had decided to use Marjorie instead of Serena, even though Serena was perfect for the part, because she couldn't stand to watch Dan moon over Serena rehearsal after rehearsal. What a mistake. It was a love scene, and Dan and Marjorie had no chemistry at all. It almost made Vanessa want to laugh when she watched it, except that she was usually already crying. That's how bad it was. She hoped the film festival judges would concentrate on the quality of the cinematography, which was her strong point, and not on the dialogue or the acting, which sucked.

Serena's film, on the other hand, had turned out to be the most austere and cerebral piece of art Vanessa had ever encountered. She could barely stand to watch it. And the most maddening thing about it was that it was completely unintentional. Serena had no clue what she was doing, but somehow the film had turned out to be completely riveting. It was pure genius. Of course part of the reason it was so good was that Vanessa had done most of the filming. She couldn't believe she'd actually helped Serena make the frigging thing without taking any credit for it at all.

Dan looked at his watch for the fiftieth time that minute. He was practically peeing in his pants he was so anxious.

"Jesus. Why don't you just call her?" Vanessa snapped impatiently. Jealousy brought out the worst in her.

Dan had programmed Serena's number into his cell phone

weeks ago. He pulled the phone out of his coat pocket and stepped off his stool, pacing back and forth as he waited for her to pick up. Finally the answering machine came on. "Hey, it's Dan. We're in Brooklyn. Where are you? Give me a call when you get a chance. Okay. 'Bye." He tried to make his voice sound nonchalant, but it was nearly impossible. Where *was* she, anyway?

He went back to his bar stool and climbed on. A steaming glass of Irish coffee sat on the bar in front of him. It was topped with a tower of whipped cream, and it smelled awesome. "She wasn't home," he said, then blew into his drink before taking a gigantic gulp.

Serena was riding up in the elevator on her way home when she realized her mistake. With her in the elevator was an elderly woman in a mink coat, clutching the Styles section of the Sunday *Times*. It was Sunday. Serena was supposed to be in Brooklyn, going over the final cut of her film with Vanessa and Jenny. And she was supposed to be there an hour ago.

"Shit," Serena muttered to herself.

The woman in the mink glared at her before stepping off the elevator. In her day, young girls living on Fifth Avenue didn't wear blue jeans or swear in public. They attended cotillions and wore gloves and pearls.

Serena could do the gloves-and-pearls thing, too. She just preferred blue jeans.

"Shit," Serena said again, tossing her keys on the table in the foyer. She hurried down the hall to her room. The answering machine light was flashing. She pressed the button and listened to Dan's message.

"Shit," she said for a third time. She hadn't been expecting Dan to be there, too. And she didn't have Dan's or Jenny's cell phone numbers, just their number at home, so she couldn't call back.

Deep down, she knew why she'd probably forgotten to go to Brooklyn. She hadn't wanted to watch her film again, especially not in front of other people. It was the first one she'd ever made, and she was a little insecure about it, although Vanessa seemed to think it was truly awesome.

It wasn't a typical sort of film. It was kind of like a film about making a film when you don't have any actors and don't know how to use the equipment. Like a documentary within a documentary. Serena had loved making it: she just wasn't sure it would make any sense to anyone who didn't know her. But Vanessa had been so enthusiastic Serena had gone ahead and entered it in Constance Billard's senior film festival. First place was a trip to the Cannes Film Festival in May, a prize donated by Isabel Coates's famous actor father.

Serena had already been to Cannes many times, so she didn't really care about the prize. But it would be cool to win, especially since both Blair and Vanessa had entered and they were both in the advanced senior film-studies class, while Serena had no experience at all in film.

Serena found her Constance Billard class list on her desk and dialed Vanessa's home number. "Hey, it's Serena," she said, when the answering machine picked up. "I completely forgot that we were meeting today. Sorry. I'm such a loser. Anyway, see you in school tomorrow, okay? 'Bye."

Next, she dialed Dan's home number.

"Hello?" a gruff voice answered.

"Is this Mr. Humphrey?" Serena asked. Unlike Serena and most of the people she knew, Dan didn't have his own phone line.

"Yes, what do you want?"

"Is Dan there?" she asked. "This is his friend, Serena."

"The one with the golden arms and raspberry lips? The one with wings for hands?"

"Excuse me?" Serena said, taken aback. Was Dan's father insane?

"He's been writing poetry about you," Mr. Humphrey said. "He left his notebook on the table."

"Oh," Serena said. "Well, can you tell him that I called?"

"Of course," Mr. Humphrey said. "I'm sure he'll be delighted."

"Thanks," Serena said. "'Bye." She hung up and began chewing on her thumbnail, a bad habit she had picked up last year at boarding school. The idea of Dan writing poetry about her made her even more nervous than the idea of him watching her film. Was Dan way, way, way more into her than she'd thought he was?

Um, yeah. He was.

"I don't think she's coming," Jenny said, yawning. "She was probably out really late last night or something." Jenny liked to think of Serena as a goddess of the night, out at all hours swilling champagne and dancing on tables.

Until recently, that would have been true.

"I'd still like to see her film, though," Dan said, brushing his shaggy hair from his eyes and grinning slyly at Vanessa. "Do you think we could go over to your place and watch it?"

Vanessa shrugged. "I'd rather not. I've watched it like four hundred times." The real truth was she couldn't stand to sit and watch Dan drool over Serena like a lovesick puppy. It was too unbearable.

"I think you should wait until Serena says it's okay,"

Jenny told Dan. "I mean, how do you know she wants you to see it?"

"She won't mind," Dan said.

Vanessa hated the giddy anticipation shining in Dan's eyes. He couldn't wait to see Serena's film. She handed him her keys. "I'm going to hang here with Clark. You guys can go watch the film if you want. It's on the VCR in Ruby's room. Don't worry, Ruby's away for the weekend."

Jenny shook her head. "I don't want to watch it without Serena," she insisted.

Dan took the keys and stood up. He was disappointed Serena hadn't shown up herself, but no way was he going to miss this. "Fine," he said. "I'll watch it alone."

Jenny swiveled from left to right on her bar stool, watching her brother leave and nursing her Coke.

"Hey, do you have Peterson for American history this year?" Vanessa asked Jenny, in an attempt to start a conversation. "People are always making shit up about how she's this big drug addict, but we had a student-teacher conference once, and she told me all about this shaky hand disease she has. It was actually really cool of her to tell me about it. She's awesome."

Jenny kept swiveling her stool. "We don't do American history until next year," she said flatly. She didn't know why Vanessa was being so nice to her all of a sudden.

Vanessa had expected a warmer welcome. "So you have European history? Sorry, I can't remember anything about ninth grade," she said.

"Yeah," Jenny responded. "It sucks." She hopped off her bar stool and fumbled with the buttons on her Diesel jean jacket. "Um, I think I'm going to grab a cab home. See you later."

"'Bye," Vanessa replied. So much for trying to be nice. She wished she could just dump Dan and his rotten little sister from her life altogether. To distract herself, she watched Clark's butt as he bent over to stock the bar fridge with more bottled beer.

"Hey boyfriend," she yelled at him. "I'm lonely."

Clark looked over his shoulder and blew her a kiss.

Thank God for Clark, Vanessa thought. If only he were more . . .

If only he were Dan.

j plays ball with the big boys

"Can you let me off here?" Jenny asked.

Her cab driver had taken the FDR uptown after the Williamsburg Bridge and was trying to cross over to the West Side at Seventy-ninth Street, but traffic was terrible and they'd been stopped at the same light for ten minutes. Jenny watched the fare on the meter go up and up while they stood still. She could have bought three new M•A•C lip glosses for what this cab ride was costing her. Finally she couldn't stand it anymore. It was a beautiful autumn day: she could walk.

She paid the driver and stepped onto the sidewalk at Seventy-ninth and Madison and headed west, toward Central Park. The November afternoon sun was low in the sky and Jenny squinted as she hurried across Fifth Avenue and into the park. Autumn leaves scattered the walkways, and the air smelled of burning firewood and hot dogs from the street vendors. Jenny kicked along the walkway with her hands stuffed into her jacket pockets, looking down at her light blue Pumas and brooding about her brother. Did he know how lame he was being? It was as though he'd completely lost his personality and was devoting every waking minute to worshipping Serena. Jenny also knew for a fact that Dan had been writing mopey, sad-ass poetry about Serena, because she'd caught him doing it.

When I cut myself shaving, I think of your teeth on my lip, and the pain becomes pleasure.

That was the line she had managed to read before Dan had snatched his notebook away. It was worse than pathetic.

The useful thing about Dan getting together with Serena was that now Jenny could walk up to Serena in school and just start talking to her, even though Serena was like, the coolest senior in New York and Jenny was a lowly ninth-grader. But if Serena ever found out how pathetically lovesick Dan was, she would run away screaming. What if Serena got so sick of Dan she wouldn't even want to talk to Jenny anymore? Dan was going to ruin everything.

Jenny wove her way through the park, not caring which direction she was walking. She reached the edge of Sheep Meadow and stepped onto the grass.

A few hundred feet away a group of boys were playing soccer. Jenny couldn't take her eyes off them—one of them in particular. His hair shone dark honey-gold in the sunlight as he dribbled the ball nimbly past his friends and shot it into the makeshift goal made up of the boys' sweaters and back-packs. His skin was tanned, and the muscles on his bare arms made Jenny want to hug herself.

Suddenly the soccer ball came sailing through the air. It landed and bounced to Jenny's feet.

She stared at it, heat creeping into her face.

"Go on, kick it!" one of the boys shouted. Jenny looked up. It was the golden boy, standing only thirty feet away, hands on his hips, his green eyes sparkling. His cheeks were flushed pink and his forehead was beaded with sweat. Jenny wanted to taste it. She'd never seen a boy look so good, or felt the way she did looking at him.

Pulling her eyes away, she concentrated on the ball, biting her lip in concentration as she drew her foot back. Then she kicked the ball as hard as she could.

Instead of rocketing back into the stretch of grass where the boys were playing, it shot straight up into the air above her head. Jenny clapped her hand over her mouth in utter mortification.

"Got it!" the golden boy shouted, sprinting toward her. The ball fell out of the sky and he headed it back to his friends, the muscles in his neck flexing magically. He stopped and turned to Jenny.

"Thanks," he said, panting. He was standing so close Jenny could smell him. He offered his hand. "I'm Nate."

Jenny stared at his hand for a second, then reached out and took it. "I'm Jennifer," she said. Jennifer sounded so much older and more sophisticated than Jenny. From now on, she promised herself, she was going to be Jennifer.

"Want to come hang out with us for a while?" Nate asked as they shook hands. Jennifer had such a sweet face, and she'd tried so hard to kick the ball, well, he couldn't resist.

"Um . . . ," Jenny said, deliberating. As she did, Nate noticed Jenny's chest. Man, was it ever huge. He couldn't let her get away, not without Jeremy and the other guys getting a chance to check her out.

Boys: they're all the same.

"Come on," he said. "We're all good guys. Promise."

Jenny glanced at the other three boys, making sure that Chuck Bass wasn't among them. Jenny had drunk a little too much champagne at a big fancy party a few weeks ago and had let a boy named Chuck Bass dance her into the ladies' room. All he did was kiss her, although he'd have done much more if Serena and Dan hadn't come to her rescue. Chuck hadn't even bothered to ask Jenny's name. What an asshole.

But Chuck Bass wasn't there.

Jenny shrugged. "Okay," she said. She couldn't believe this was happening. She'd heard of a Nate from parties and school gossip, and she was sure this had to be the same Nate. He was the most beautiful boy on the Upper East Side, and he had just asked *her* to hang out! It was as if she'd walked into the other side of the wardrobe and entered a world of fantasy-come-true, leaving her lame, lovesick brother and his stupid-ass poetry far, far behind.

Nate led Jenny over to his friends, who had stopped playing ball and were sitting on the grass, drinking blue Gatorade.

"Guys, this is Jennifer," Nate said, with a happy smile on his face. "Jennifer, this is Jeremy, Charlie, and Anthony."

Jenny smiled at the boys, and the boys smiled at her chest. "Nice to meet you, Jennifer," Jeremy Scott Tomkinson said appreciatively. He was small and skinny, and his khakis had grass stains on them. He had a great haircut though, with long sideburns and thick bangs, like an English rock star.

"Come. Join us," Anthony Avuldsen said in his classic stoner voice. His hair was light blond and his nose was sprinkled with adorable freckles. His arm muscles were even bigger than Nate's, but Jenny preferred Nate's.

"We were just about to light up," Charlie Dern said, brandishing a little pipe. His head was a mess of unruly brown hair, and he was monumentally tall. Sitting cross-legged, his knees were practically up to his ears. In his lap was a little plastic baggie full of pot.

"You don't mind, do you, Jennifer?" Nate asked.

Jenny shrugged, trying to look nonchalant, even though

she was a little nervous. She'd never smoked pot before. "Of course not," she said.

She and Nate sat down on the grass with the other boys. Charlie lit the pipe, inhaled deeply, and passed it to Nate.

Jenny studied the way Nate held the pipe. She wanted to try it, but she didn't want them to know it was her first time.

Nate's cheeks were full of smoke as he passed the pipe to Jenny. She cupped it in her left hand and brought it to her lips, just as he had done. Nate lit the bowl for her, flicking the lighter a few times before it caught. Then she inhaled. She could feel the smoke filling up her lungs, but she wasn't sure what to do with it.

"'Ere," Jenny said, desperately trying to hold in the smoke. She passed the pipe to Anthony.

"Nice hit," Charlie remarked, nodding approvingly at her.

Jenny's eyes were tearing. "Tanks," she said, letting a little smoke seep out the corners of her lips.

"Jesus, this stuff is strong," Nate said, shaking his golden head.

"Whew," Jenny said in agreement, finally blowing out the rest of the smoke. She felt extremely cool.

The pipe made its way back to her, and this time she lit it herself, copying the way the boys had done it, while trying to look casual. Again, she held in the smoke for as long as she could bear to without coughing. Her eyeballs felt like they were going to explode.

"This reminds me of something," she said, passing the pipe to Anthony once more. "I can't remember what, but it's definitely something."

"Yeah," Jeremy agreed.

"It reminds me of summer," Anthony said.

"No, that's not it," Jenny said, closing her eyes. Her father had sent her to a hippie arts camp in the Adirondack Mountains for the summer. She'd had to write haikus about the environment, sing peace songs in Spanish and Chinese, and weave blankets for the homeless. The entire place smelled like pee and peanut butter. "My summer sucked. What I'm thinking of is something good, like Halloween when you're a little kid."

"Definitely," said Nate. He lay back in the grass and looked up at the orange autumn leaves fluttering in the trees overhead. "It's exactly like Halloween," he said.

Jenny lay down next to him. Normally she never would have done such a thing, because when she lay down, her boobs oozed over the sides of her ribcage and bulged out of her clothing in a deformed manner. But for once she wasn't worried about her boobs. It felt nice just to lie there beside Nate, breathing the same air that he was breathing.

"When I was little I used to cover my eyes and think no one could see me if I couldn't see them," she said, passing her hand over her eyes.

"Me too," Nate said, closing his eyes. He felt completely relaxed, like a dog napping in front of the fire after a long run. This Jennifer girl was genuinely nice and so completely without expectation; it felt great to be with her.

If only Blair knew how easy it was to make him happy.

"When you're younger, everything is pretty simple like that, you know?" Jenny said. Her tongue felt loose in her mouth, and she couldn't stop talking. "Then the older you get, the more complicated things are."

"Completely," Nate said. "Like getting into college. All of a sudden we have to plan what we're doing for the rest of our lives and try to impress people with how smart and involved we are. I mean, do our parents take eight classes a day, play on sports teams, edit the paper, and tutor underprivileged children, or whatever every single day? No."

"It's crazy," Jenny agreed. She had yet to feel the pressure of getting into college, but she could empathize. "I mean, all my dad does all day is read and listen to the radio. How come we have to do so much?"

"I don't know." Nate sighed tiredly. He reached for Jenny's hand and wound his fingers around hers.

Jenny felt as if she were melting into the grass. The side of her that was next to Nate was warm and humming, and her hand felt like it had fused to his. She'd never felt so wonderful in her entire life.

"Hey, do you want to come over to my house and get something to eat?" Nate said, rubbing his thumb over her knuckles.

Jenny nodded. She knew she didn't have to say anything. Nate could hear her.

She couldn't believe how quickly life could change. How could she have known when she'd woken up that morning that today was the day she'd fall in love?

d is obsessed

Dan felt a little perverted at first, watching Serena's film all alone in Vanessa and Ruby's apartment. But as soon as he'd gotten himself a glass of Coke from their old brown fridge, settled on the end of Ruby's unmade futon bed, and pressed play, he'd forgotten about feeling self-conscious.

The camera zoomed in on Serena's glossy, red lips. "Welcome to my world," she said, laughing. Then her lips started walking. Or rather, Serena herself was walking. The camera stayed focused on her lips while the background changed. "I'm hailing a cab," Serena said. "I take so many cabs. It's expensive."

A cab stopped behind her and the lips got into the backseat. "We're heading downtown now. To Jeffrey. It's a great store. I don't know what I'm looking for, but I'm sure I'll find it."

The camera remained on her lips, which were silent for the entire ride. Music played. Something '60s and French. Serge Gainsbourg, maybe. Glimpses of New York street scenes were visible through the smudged cab window.

Dan clutched his glass of Coke. It was such a tease to only see Serena's lips. He felt like he was going to pass out.

"We're here," Serena's lips said finally. The camera followed her lips out of the cab and through the large glass entryway of a bright, white store. "Look at all these fabulous clothes," the lips murmured. They remained slightly parted as Serena took in the contents of the store. "I'm in heaven."

Dan fumbled in his pants pocket for a cigarette, his hands shaking uncontrollably. He smoked one and then another as the camera patrolled the store along with Serena's lips, stopping first to kiss a tiny brown handbag with a picture of a dog on it and then to drag a pair of sequined angora arm-warmers across the camera's lens. Finally her lips discovered a dress that they just couldn't get enough of.

"It's so perfectly red," her lips said in awe. "I'm way into red these days. Okay. I'm trying it on."

Dan lit a third cigarette.

The camera followed Serena's lips into the dressing room. They chattered away as Serena removed her clothes. "It's freezing in here," she said. "I hope this isn't too small. I hate it when things are too small." Her hair, her bare shoulders, her neck, her ear were all visible in the mirror for a fraction of a second, but nothing was in focus. It was almost unbearable to watch.

And then . . .

"Ta da!" the lips said. The camera panned back slowly, revealing Serena in her entirety, sporting a gorgeous, strappy red dress. Her feet were bare and her toes were painted red, too. "Isn't it amazing?" she said, clapping her hands and spinning around and around, the dress flaring out around her knees. The French song came on again, and then the picture faded to black.

Dan fell back on the bed. He felt drugged. More than anything he wanted to be with Serena right now. Those lips! He wanted to kiss them again and again.

He dug his cell phone out of his coat pocket and pressed

the buttons to search for her number, hitting send when he found it.

"Hello?" Serena picked up after the first ring.

"It's Dan," he said, his voice cracking. He could barely breathe.

"Hey. I'm so, so, so sorry I forgot to come meet you guys. Was Vanessa totally pissed or what?"

Dan closed his eyes. "I just watched your film," he said. He reached for the remote and hit rewind.

Serena paused. *How embarrassing.* "Oh," she said. "What'd you think?"

Dan took a deep breath. "I think—" Could he say it? Could he? All it took was three words. He could say them right now and be done with it. He could.

But he couldn't.

"I loved . . . it," he said instead, chickening out on the last word.

"Really?"

"Uh-huh."

"Well, what does your sister think? She's only seen bits and pieces of it. There was tons more film, but Vanessa and I finally streamlined it down to just the lips thing."

"Jenny didn't want to watch it without you," Dan said. "It's just me here. Vanessa gave me the key." He felt weird admitting this, but he didn't want to lie.

"Oh," Serena said, remembering what Dan's father had said about Dan writing poetry about her. Now he was watching her film all alone in Vanessa's house? Serena didn't want to feel weird about it, but it was hard not to.

"I'm really psyched for next weekend," Dan said, sitting up. "Do you think I should try and schedule an interv—?"

"Cool," Serena said, cutting him off. "So I'll see you Friday, right? Grand Central, three o'clock."

"Okay," Dan said. Was that it? They were done talking?

"'Bye," Serena said and hung up. She didn't want to linger on the phone in case Dan said something intense she couldn't handle. Things were already far more intense than she'd intended.

"'Bye," Dan said. He pressed play on the remote once more, his brain still fuzzy from the spell the film had cast. It couldn't hurt to watch it again, could it?

Hmm . . . Anyone smell obsession? And we're not talking about the perfume.

smooth sailing

"I've never been inside a house like this," Jenny said, standing on the stoop of Nate's town house. It was three stories high, with green-painted window boxes filled with geraniums, and ivy cascading from the roof. The door had a complicated series of alarms and locks, and a security camera was trained on the house front and back.

Nate shrugged as he punched a code into the alarm system. "It's just like living in an apartment," he said. "Except there are stairs."

"Yeah," Jenny said. "I guess." She didn't want to let on how truly awestruck she was.

Nate led her inside. The foyer floor was made of red marble. A giant stone lion stood in one corner. Someone had put a fur hat on its head. Down a set of stairs was an enormous sunken living room. There were original oil paintings by famous artists on every wall. Jenny even thought she recognized some of them. Renoir. Sargent. Picasso.

"My parents are into art," Nate said when he noticed Jenny staring. Then he noticed something else. A wrapped package sat on the side table. The card had his name on it. Nate went over to it and ripped open the envelope.

BLAIR PAIGE WALDORF was printed on the face of the card in classic Tiffany letterhead. Inside it read: *For Nate. You know I love you. Blair.*

"What's that?" Jenny said. "Is it your birthday or something?"

"Nah," Nate said. He stuffed the card back in its envelope, picked up the box, and stashed it on the floor of the coat closet. He wasn't even curious about what was inside. It was probably just a sweater or some cologne. Blair was always giving him stuff for no reason, except to get attention. She could be so demanding sometimes.

"So what do you want to eat?" he asked Jenny, leading her down the hall and into the kitchen. "Our cook makes awesome brownies. I bet there are still some left."

"Cook?" Jenny echoed, following him. "Of course you have a cook."

Nate located a cookie tin on top of the enormous marble kitchen counter and opened it. He pulled out a brownie and shoved it in his mouth. "My mom's not exactly the best cook in the world," he said. The idea of his mother even making toast was a complete joke. She was a French princess who lived on restaurant food or catered meals at dinner parties. She'd barely even been in the kitchen.

"Try one," Nate said. He handed Jenny a brownie.

"Thanks." Jenny took the brownie even though she was too excited to eat it. It was going to melt in her sticky palm.

"Let's go upstairs," Nate said. "This way's fastest."

Jenny sucked in her breath. She had never been alone with a boy in his house before, and it was a little scary. But she wanted to trust Nate. He was so unlike that horrible Chuck Bass who had taken advantage of her at that party. Chuck had seemed dangerous and exciting at first, but he'd never even asked Jenny what her name was. Nate was polite. He seemed genuinely interested in getting to know her. And Jenny was genuinely interested in letting him.

Nate led Jenny out a side door and up a narrow stairwell. She had read enough Jane Austen and Henry James books to know that these were the servants' stairs. On the third floor Nate opened the door at the top of the stairs onto a wide hallway lit overhead by a glass skylight. They passed an oil portrait of a little boy dressed in a sailor outfit and holding a wooden boat. It was Nate, Jenny realized.

Nate opened another door. "This is my room."

Jenny followed him inside. Other than the antique sleigh bed and the ultramodern, ultracool desk with a wafer-thin laptop sitting on it, his room looked pretty normal. The bed was covered with a green-and-black plaid flannel comforter; there were DVDs scattered on the floor, dumbbells stacked precariously in a corner, shoes spilling out of the closet, and vintage Beatles posters hanging on the walls.

"It's nice," Jenny said, sitting down nervously on the edge of the bed. She noticed the model of a sailboat sitting on the bedside table. "Do you sail?"

"Yeah," Nate said, picking up the model boat. "Me and my dad make boats. Up in Maine." He handed the model to Jenny. "This is the one we're working on now. It's a cruiser, so it's got a heavier hull than the boats we build to race with. We're going to sail it to the Caribbean first. And then maybe even to Europe."

"Really?" Jenny examined the model boat. She couldn't imagine sailing across the Atlantic in something so small and delicate. "Does it have a toilet?"

Nate smiled. "Yeah. Here." He stuck his pinky down into the cabin. There was a tiny oval door with the letters *WC* printed on it. "See it?"

Jenny nodded in fascination. "I'd love to know how to sail," she said.

Nate sat down next to her. "Maybe you could come up to Maine and I could teach you," he said quietly.

Jenny turned to him, her big brown eyes searching his emerald green ones. "I'm only fourteen," she said.

Nate reached up and touched her curly brown hair, combing it ever so gently with his fingers. Then he put his hand down again. "I know," he said. "It's okay."

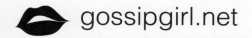

Disclaimer: All the real names of places, people, and events have been altered or abbreviated to protect the innocent. Namely, me.

hey people!

EVERYBODY'S DOING IT

Even I am guilty of having taken an extra Kit Kat from the newsstand on the corner back in fifth grade. I did it on a dare, but I still have guilt-ridden nightmares about it. You don't see me taking purses from Prada or undies from Armani. But some girls can't help themselves.

Winona Ryder got caught stealing some nice clothes in an LA boutique. Claimed it was research for a role she was playing. Yeah, right. And Now **B**. She was even good enough at it not to get caught.

Of course what they stole is totally critical. It wouldn't be very cool for them to have stolen, say, some duct tape from Ace Hardware or toilet paper from CVS. But a pair of cashmere pajamas? That's majorly high class. It's also majorly psychotic. Next thing you know, **B** will be stealing Jaguars and Mercedes-Benzes!

Sightings

B dropping off a wrapped present at **N**'s town house. **N** wasn't home, so she gave it to the maid. **D** leaving **V**'s apartment in Brooklyn and walking almost all the way home to the Upper West Side. Now that's a long walk. Guess he needed to chill out. **S** biting her nails and reading *No Exit* in **The Corner Bookstore** on Ninety-third and Madison. Trying to understand **D** a little better, maybe. Little **J** leaving **N**'s house with a perma-grin plastered to her face. Love is a many-splendored thing. Careful, **J**—the Waspoid is not the most reliable breed to fall in love with.

For those who don't know . . . Waspoid: *noun*. The elite version of the wasteoid, or stoner boy. Wears cashmere sweaters. Likes to smoke pot—a lot. Doesn't like to commit. But maybe **N** will surprise us.

Your E-Mail

Q: Dear GG,
What do you think about older boys dating younger girls?
—Sneaky

A: Dear Sneaky,
It definitely depends on the age difference and the circumstances. For instance, if you were a college senior dating a high school sophomore I would say you had a bit of a Woody Allen-Soon Yi Previn problem. If you were a high school senior dating a college freshman, that would be okay. A high school senior dating a high school freshman is pushing it. It seems to work better when the girl is the younger one, mainly because we mature much faster—in all ways.
—GG

Q: Dear Gossip Girl,
I'm pretty sure I saw **B** stealing a bottle of Aveda shampoo from Zitomer. I mean, it's not like she doesn't have any money. If she had any real friends, they'd get her some help.
—Spygirl

A: Dear Spygirl,
Thanks for the tip. The truth is, I don't think shoplifting is **B**'s biggest problem right now. Have you seen the guy who's about to become her new stepdad?
—GG

THE CONSTANCE BILLARD SCHOOL SENIOR FILM FESTIVAL AWARDS

V, B, and *S* have all entered. *V* with her little piece of *War and Peace; B* with a redo of the first ten minutes of *Breakfast at Tiffany's;* and *S* with her . . . *thing.* Competition is high. Both *V* and *B* think they have it in the bag. *S* doesn't think she has a chance. I'm taking bets!

You know you love me,

gossip girl

b and v can't wait to graduate

"Where's it going to be?"

"How many guests is she having?"

"How many bridesmaids?"

"What are you going to wear?"

"How many layers is she having on the cake?"

"Is your father invited?"

Blair held her breath. It was lunchtime, and she was waiting in line with Kati and Isabel in the Constance Billard School cafeteria. Blair wasn't even hungry, not anymore. Kati had started the whole annoying inquisition by mentioning that she'd seen a really cool wedding dress in a '60s *Vogue* she'd found in a thrift shop. The dress had little crystal daisies all over it, white velvet trim, and a big white velvet bow in the back. Then Isabel had asked Blair if her mother was going to wear a traditional white wedding dress or something different. Now Blair was surrounded by eager Constance girls with Monday-bright eyes, all firing questions at her about her mother's wedding. To her disgust, her senior classmates weren't the only ones who thought they had a right to know all the boring details. Becky Dormand and her group of annoying junior followers were practically pulling on Blair's black cashmere sweater, drooling over any tidbit of wedding news. Even a few bold ninth-graders were lingering nearby, hoping to hear enough to brag about it to their friends.

"It's really not such a big deal," Blair said impatiently. "She's been married before, you know."

"Who are the bridesmaids?" Becky Dormand asked.

"Me, Kati, Isabel . . ." Blair slid her lunch tray along the cafeteria counter and picked up a coffee yogurt. "Serena and my aunts," she added quickly.

Fudge-frosted brownies on little white plates sat temptingly on a shelf at eye-level. She picked one up, examined it for any defects, and then put it on her tray. Even if she actually decided to eat it, she could always throw it up later.

It wasn't much, but at least she had *that* much control over her life.

"Serena?" Becky repeated, glancing at her groupies in shocked surprise. "Really?"

"Yes," Blair snapped. "Really."

If it weren't for the fact that she was head of Constance's social services board, leader of the French club, and chairwoman of all the worthwhile junior social functions in the city, Blair would have told Becky to fuck off. But Blair was a role model: she had a reputation to uphold.

She tossed a few leaves of spinach onto a plate and slopped some bleu cheese dressing on top of them. Then she picked up her tray and headed into the cafeteria. Grades one through eight had already eaten, so the room was filled with uniformed upper-school girls gossiping about each other and picking at their food.

"I heard Blair is getting liposuction before the wedding just to make sure she looks good in *Vogue*," snitched a junior girl to her friends.

"I thought she already had it," quipped another girl. "Isn't that why she always wears black tights? To hide the scars?"

"I heard Nate is cheating on her, but Blair won't break up with him before they get their pictures taken together at the wedding," Becky Dormand said, joining them. "Isn't that so typical?"

Serena van der Woodsen was sitting alone reading a book at the table where Blair usually sat. Serena had pulled her blond hair up into a bun, and she was wearing a black V-neck sweater with nothing underneath it. Her legs were crossed, and her short maroon wool uniform actually looked stylish. She looked like a model for Burberry or Miu Miu.

Actually, she looked better than a model because she wasn't *trying* to look good: she just did.

Blair turned away and headed for a table by the windows. Just because her mother had asked Serena to be a bridesmaid didn't mean she had to talk to her.

When they were younger, Blair and Serena had taken baths together. They'd had sleepovers every weekend, during which they practiced kissing on pillows, made prank calls to their nerdy seventh-grade bio teacher, and stayed up all night giggling. Serena had been there for Blair when she got her period at the end of eighth grade and was terrified of tampons. They'd gotten drunk for the first time together. And they'd both loved Nate like a brother. At least at first.

But Serena had gone away to boarding school two years ago and spent all of her vacations partying in Europe, sending Blair only the occasional postcard. It had been especially hurtful when Blair's father had announced he was gay and her mother had sued him for divorce. Blair had had no one to turn to.

There was also the small matter that Serena and Nate had already slept together, while Blair and Nate still hadn't.

So when Serena had returned to the city, Blair had

decided to pay her back by ignoring her and demanding that all their other friends ignore Serena, too. She had turned Serena into a social leper.

Blair sat down and began poking angrily at her salad. After she'd left Barneys the day before, she'd sat on a park bench for a while, waiting for Serena to clear out of the area. When she finally returned home, her mother informed her that she'd just closed her bank account and opened a new joint account with Cyrus. Blair's new credit card would be coming in a day or two. That explained why her credit card didn't work. Thanks for the update, Mom.

Blair had found a nice box in her closet to put the pajama bottoms in. She wrapped it in pretty silver paper and tied it with a black bow, and then she took it over to Nate's house. But Nate hadn't called last night to thank her. What was his problem, anyway?

Kati and Isabel sat down across from Blair.

"Why don't you just tell your mom you don't *want* Serena to be a bridesmaid?" Isabel reasoned. She wound her thick brown hair into a knot on top of her head and took a sip of skim milk. "I'm sure she'd listen to you."

"Just tell your mom you and Serena aren't friends anymore," Kati put in. She picked a frizzy blond hair out of her tea. Her hair always got all over everything.

Blair stole a glance at Serena. She knew her mother had already talked to Serena's mother and that Serena already knew that she was supposed to be a bridesmaid. Tempting as it was, she couldn't ask her mother to *un*ask her. That would be tacky. And Blair didn't want to risk giving Serena anything to complain about, just in case Serena *had* seen her take those pajamas in Barneys. Serena might smear her name all over the Upper East Side.

"It's too late," Blair said and shrugged. "I'm really not that bothered by it. She's just going to walk into the church with us wearing the same dress, or whatever. It's not like we have to hang out together."

That wasn't exactly true. Her mother was planning some sort of luncheon and a day of beauty for all the bridesmaids, but Blair was pretending that that wasn't happening.

"So what do the dresses look like? Have you and your mom picked anything out yet?" Kati asked, biting into her brownie. "Please tell me we don't have to wear anything tight. I promised myself I'd lose ten pounds before Christmas, but look at me eating this stupid brownie!"

Blair rolled her eyes and stirred up her yogurt. "Who cares what we wear?" she said.

Isabel and Kati stared at her. Neither of them could believe she'd just said that. *Of course* it mattered.

When a girl like Blair says a thing like that, you know something is up.

Blair took a bite of her yogurt, ignoring them. What was wrong with everyone anyway? Couldn't they just shut up about the wedding and leave her alone?

"I'm not really hungry," she said, suddenly standing up. "I think I'm going to go send some e-mails or something."

Kati pointed to the untouched brownie on Blair's tray. "Aren't you going to eat that?" she asked.

Blair shook her head.

Kati picked up the brownie and put it on Isabel's tray. "We can share it," she said.

Isabel scowled and tossed the brownie back at Kati. "If you want to eat it, you take it," she insisted.

Blair picked up her tray and hurried away. She couldn't wait to fucking graduate.

★   ★   ★

Jenny spotted Serena the instant she walked into the cafeteria with her cup of tea and her banana. She was sitting alone, reading something. Jenny hurried over.

"Is it okay if I sit with you?" she asked.

"Of course," Serena said, closing her book. It was *The Sorrows of Young Werther,* by Goethe. Jenny had never heard of it.

Serena caught her looking at the book. "Your brother recommended it to me. I honestly don't know how he can read this shit. It's seriously boring." Actually, Dan hadn't recommended the book to her, but he'd mentioned that he'd read it. It was all about a guy who was totally obsessed with a girl. She was all he thought about and all he could write about. It was kind of creepy.

Jenny laughed. "You should see some of the poetry he writes," she said.

Serena frowned. She wished she *could* see some of the poetry Dan had written, since supposedly some of it was about her.

She closed the book. "Promise you won't tell on me if I don't finish this?" she said.

"I won't say anything," Jenny promised. "As long as you promise not to tell him I told you his poetry was boring."

"I promise," Serena said.

Jenny sneaked a peek under the table. As usual, Serena was wearing the maroon polyester-blend pleated kilt, the uniform unofficially reserved for seventh-grade losers. Except she looked amazing in it. She always looked amazing. "You know, you're like, the only senior who wears the maroon uniform," Jenny remarked.

Serena shrugged. "I think it's cool," she said. "Navy blue is boring, and wearing the gray one makes you never want to wear gray again in your life, and I like gray."

Jenny was wearing the gray uniform. "I guess you're right," she said. "I have a pair of gray pants I never wear. Maybe that's why." She cleared her throat. What she really wanted to talk to Serena about was Nate.

"Hey, sorry I messed up yesterday," Serena said. "I forgot all about meeting up with you and Vanessa."

"That's okay," Jenny started to say. "As it turned out, I had an amazing—"

"Hey guys," Vanessa Abrams said, walking up to their table. She was wearing black tights that did their best to hide her chunky knees. "What's up?"

"Hey. Sorry about yesterday," Serena said.

Vanessa shrugged. "That's okay. I'm sort of sick of watching those films over and over anyway." *Especially your film,* she thought bitterly. *It's too fucking good.*

Serena nodded. "Grab a chair."

Jenny glared at Vanessa. She wanted Serena all to herself.

"Sorry, I can't," Vanessa said. "Um, Jenny, we really have to get going developing film for this month's *Rancor* feature. There's like twenty rolls of it, and the dark room's totally free right now. Do you think you could help me out?"

Jenny glanced at Serena, who shrugged and stood up. "I should get going anyway," she said. "I have a college meeting with Ms. Glos. Fun, fun, fun."

"I just had mine," Vanessa said. "Watch out, she's having another bloody nose."

Ms. Glos had yellow-tinged skin and frequent bloody noses. All the girls were convinced she had some terrible contagious disease. If she gave you a handout or loaned you a college catalog, you had to wear gloves when you read it. Either that or wash your hands in very hot water afterward.

"Great," Serena giggled. "Okay, I'll see you guys later."

Vanessa sat down and waited for Jenny to finish eating her banana.

Jenny took the last bite and folded the peel up into a paper napkin.

"Ready?" Vanessa said.

Jenny shrugged. "Actually, I can't. I have a history paper to print out for next period. Sorry," she said, standing up.

Vanessa frowned. "Fine," she said. "But let me know when you're free. I really do need help."

"Okay," Jenny said breezily. "I'll let you know. Oh, and do you think you could call me Jennifer, instead of Jenny, from now on? I'd really prefer it."

Vanessa stared at her. "Okay. Jennifer."

"Thanks," Jenny said, and hurried off to the computer room. Maybe Nate had e-mailed her!

Vanessa watched Jenny leave, wondering how she had turned into such a royal bitch. She'd thought hanging out with Jenny would make her feel closer to Dan, but it had only pissed her off. Jenny was just like all the other six-hundred-odd girls at Constance—shallow and stuck up.

Vanessa, too, could not wait to fucking graduate.

amor omnia vincit

Instant Message
From: <u>Bwaldorf@constancebillard.edu</u>
To: <u>Narchibald@St.Judes.edu</u>

<u>Bwaldorf</u>: hey natie
<u>Bwaldorf</u>: i'm going insane here. everyone
wants to talk about the wedding,
as if i could give a fuck.
<u>Bwaldorf</u>: nate? i know you're online. are
you meeting me after French club
today or what?
<u>Bwaldorf</u>: did you get the present i left
for you yesterday?
<u>Bwaldorf</u>: hello????
<u>Bwaldorf</u>: fine.

Instant Message
From: <u>Narchibald@St.Judes.edu</u>
To: <u>Jhumphrey@constancebillard.edu</u>
<u>Narchibald</u>: hey Jennifer.
<u>Jhumphrey</u>: hey

<u>Narchibald</u>:	want to meet me in the park after school?
<u>Jhumphrey</u>:	um, ok. what are we doing?
<u>Narchibald</u>:	I don't know. what do you want to do?
<u>Jhumphrey</u>:	i dunno. will ur friends be there?
<u>Narchibald</u>:	no, just me. still want to come?
<u>Jhumphrey</u>:	definitely. I can meet u outside ur school if u want.
<u>Narchibald</u>:	just meet me in front of the Met.
<u>Jhumphrey</u>:	okay, see u then.

Jenny logged off, feeling even cooler than ever. She was still only a ninth-grader, but her name was Jennifer, and after school she was meeting Nate, the hottest senior boy in the entire city. She was going to have to blow off helping Vanessa with *Rancor,* but it was completely worth it. If she were Dan, she'd write a lovesick poem about how gorgeous Nate was and how twisted fate could be, bringing two people who had nothing in common together. How it was destined for tragedy. But Jenny was more of an optimist. She satisfied herself by writing *Mrs. Jennifer Archibald* in her best calligraphy on the back of the gray mouse pad she was using.

Don't laugh. That's what ninth-graders do when they're in love.

Across town at Riverside Prep, Jenny's brother Dan was at that very moment e-mailing Serena his latest love poem, entitled "The Last Time I Died."

Your rope snug around my neck, I jumped.
Your lips kissed me as I fell, and falling still

"Come on, freak," his friend Zeke Freedman called from the door of the computer lab. "We're late for Latin."

Amo ergo sum, Dan thought. *I love therefore I am.*

"I'm busy," he said. He typed in Serena's e-mail address at Constance.

"Well, I don't want detention," said Zeke, leaving. "Want to play some b-ball in the park later?"

"Fine," Dan answered, distracted. "I'll see you there." He began constructing a brief e-mail to send along with his attachment.

```
Dear Serena,
     This weekend is going to be awesome. I
got an interview set up for Saturday, and
my dad's giving me some extra cash. I
can't wait.
     I attached a poem here. Just something
I wrote this morning. Hope you like it.
     I'll be in the basketball court near
the Meadow if you want to hang out after
school.

                    Love,
                    Dan


Amor omnia vincit! Love conquers all.
```

d turns stalkeresque

Jenny stood in front of the Met steps, trying not to be grossed out by the guy lying on the steps behind her. His pants were pulled down, and she was pretty sure his penis was hanging out.

You get used to seeing this stuff when you live in the city, but it's still seriously gross.

She really wanted to move, but Nate had told her to wait there, and Jenny didn't want to risk missing him.

"Take a hike!" the penis man shouted at a tourist.

A hot-dog vendor on the sidewalk nearby was talking on his cell phone. Jenny edged closer so she could listen, hoping he was calling the cops. But it sounded more like he was talking to his mother or something because all he said was, "Fine," over and over.

Someone touched her shoulder. "Hey, Jennifer."

Jenny wheeled around. "Hey," she said, smiling up at Nate. Her hands rose self-consciously to her face, pushing her unruly brown curls behind her ears. "I'm glad you're here. That guy was freaking me out."

"Yeah," Nate said. He put his arm around her. "Come on, let's get out of here."

At his touch, all the blood rushed to Jenny's brain. "Okay," she gasped, leaning into Nate's arm. "Let's go."

Nate kept his arm around her as they headed into the park, winding their way to Sheep Meadow. They found a nice sunny place in the grass and sat down facing each other, cross-legged, with their knees touching. It felt so nice Jenny was having trouble believing she wasn't dreaming. Out of all the girls in the entire city Nate liked *her*. It was incredible.

"I hope you don't mind, my friends are going to meet us here in little while," Nate said, pulling a bag of pot from his pocket.

Jenny shrugged. "I don't mind," she said, although she was a teensy bit disappointed. Warily, she watched Nate pull a few tufts of weed from the bag and sprinkle them into a rolling paper. Then he expertly rolled a tight little joint and licked the paper to seal it.

He offered it to Jenny and she shook her head. "I'm okay," she said. She knew it might sound lame, but she already felt a little out of it, sitting so close to Nate. She didn't want to lose her head completely.

"That's cool," Nate said. He dropped the joint into the bag and stuffed it back into his coat pocket.

Jenny blew out a small breath of relief. She wanted to get to know Nate when he was just Nate, not when he was all baked.

"So, have you been visiting colleges on the weekends and stuff?" Jenny asked. "Deciding where you want to go?"

"Yeah," Nate said, frowning. "But I'm also thinking about maybe taking a year or two off. Going sailing with my dad. I might even try to get on a team for the America's Cup."

"Wow," Jenny said, impressed. "That sounds amazing."

"Maybe I'll take three years off and we can go to college

together," Nate said, taking her hand. She had the smallest fingers.

Jenny caught Nate's gaze and they smiled at each other for a moment.

He let his head roll forward and it fell onto her shoulder. She smelled like clean laundry. "Mmmn," he said. He couldn't get over how comfortable he felt with her. He usually had to smoke up or have a few drinks before meeting Blair, just to deal with her constant planning and nagging about the future. But with Jennifer he didn't even need to be high.

Oh my God, Jenny thought. *He's about to kiss me.*

She closed her eyes. Her whole body felt tingly. Nate's head was warm, and he smelled like pine needles.

"Jennifer," Nate murmured sleepily. He lifted his head and shook his honey gold hair. "This feels nice." His eyes roamed around her face, finally settling on her lips.

Jenny giggled. He was definitely about to kiss her.

"Yo, Archibald!" somebody shouted. "Save some for us!"

Whoa. Seriously bad timing.

Jenny and Nate both turned to see Anthony, Jeremy, and Charlie loping across the grass. Jeremy was carrying a soccer ball. Nate stood up quickly, backing away from Jenny.

"Hey," he greeted his friends casually. "You made it."

"Hey guys," Jenny said, standing up slowly and brushing the stray bits of grass from her school uniform. She wished they hadn't come.

"So are you going to roll us up a big fattie or what?" Anthony said, nodding at the plastic bag hanging out of Nate's pocket.

Nate shook his head. "I'm already baked like a loaf of bread, man," he lied. He pulled the bag out of his pocket and tossed it to Anthony. "There's one rolled already."

"Thanks," Anthony said. He plunked down on the grass and got to work. "Man, do I need this," he said under his breath. "Freaking college advisor has been up my ass for the last hour."

"Tell me about it," Jeremy agreed.

Jenny bit her nails, feeling a little left out. She looked at Nate, but he had grabbed the soccer ball out of Jeremy's hands and was busy dribbling it between his feet.

"That's nothing. My dad's been up my ass about college since eighth grade," Charlie said. "He's already talked to some dean at Yale Law School, like, getting them ready for me to show up there. It's like, hey Dad, slow down!"

"So we're still going up to Brown this weekend, right?" Jeremy said.

Brown. Jenny snapped to attention. That was where Dan and Serena were going this weekend.

"Definitely," Nate said.

He passed the ball to Jenny and she kicked it softly back to him, smiling to let him know that she really didn't mind that his friends had come, or that they were all talking about college while she was only a ninth-grader. She liked knowing that Nate wasn't actually as baked as a loaf of bread, and that he'd told her he was thinking about taking some time off before college. She already knew more about him than his best friends did!

"Come on," Nate said. "Let's play ball."

She just wished Nate had kissed her after all, and that he hadn't stopped when his friends showed up.

Dan sat on a bench to wait for Zeke and Serena. Well, Zeke was definitely coming. And if Serena showed up, Dan would tell Zeke to get the hell out of there and leave them alone.

That's what friends are for.

Dan pulled a Camel out of his pocket and stuck it between his lips. His hands were shaking, partly because he'd drunk six cups of coffee since lunch, and partly because he was nervous at the prospect of seeing Serena again, especially if she'd read his poem. He pulled his writing notebook out of his pocket and stared at the last few lines of the poem without seeing them. Any minute now Serena was going to rush up and throw her arms around his neck, kissing him breathlessly and crying because it was so heartless of her not to show up on Saturday, and telling him over and over that she loved his poem. That she loved *him*.

Or not.

Dan inhaled too quickly and nearly coughed up a lung. Then he lit another cigarette with the one he was already smoking. He was going to chain-smoke until she showed up. He might be dead when she got there, but at least they'd be together.

Puffing away, he stared across the grass. A short girl with big boobs and curly brown hair was playing soccer with four boys he recognized only vaguely. It was his sister, Jenny. Since when did she hang out in the park with those boring, preppy, Upper East Side assholes? And was that guy, Chuck the Pervert, with them? Feeling protective, Dan started to stand up, but then he forced himself to sit back down again. Jenny looked like she was having a good time, and he could see Chuck wasn't there. If he wanted to be an asshole older brother, he could go over there and ruin everything, or he could just sit tight and let Jenny have her fun. He could still watch her from where he was sitting. And besides, Jenny needed to meet new people, especially now that he was seeing Serena and had less time for her.

Well, sort of seeing Serena. If she ever showed up.

"Hey, I'd really better head home," Jenny said, dribbling the ball over to Nate.

"Okay, I'll talk to you soon." He put his hand behind her head, and kissed her on the cheek.

Jenny nearly toppled over. "'Bye," she squeaked, waving to the other three boys. Then she turned and walked quickly toward Central Park West before she could pee in her pants. She couldn't wait to see Nate again. *Alone.*

"Dude, what does Blair think about your new little girl-friend?" Anthony asked Nate when Jenny had gone. He lit another joint, took a hit, and passed it to Jeremy.

"She's not my girlfriend, man," Nate said. "She's just a cool kid I stumbled into." He shrugged. "I like her."

"I like her, too," Jeremy said, passing the joint to Nate. "But Blair would not be happy if she knew you were hanging out with some ninth-grade chick instead of her. Right?"

Nate took the joint and inhaled deeply. "She doesn't have to know," he grunted, holding in the smoke. Then he exhaled. "Dude, it's not like I'm going to ditch Blair for Jennifer. It's no big deal."

"No big deal," Charlie agreed, taking the joint.

Nate watched the ember burn on the end of the joint. He knew what he'd said wasn't true. It *was* a big deal. He just wasn't sure how to handle it.

A guy had to tread carefully when a girl like Blair was involved. He'd seen what she could do, and it wasn't pretty.

"Sorry I'm late, loser," Zeke said, bouncing a basketball against Dan's head. "Come on, let's play."

Dan looked up from his notebook. He'd started another poem called "Broken Feet."

Splintered wood, flat tires, broken glass.
Fate wields its unfair axe. Collapse.

It was about wanting to be somewhere with someone and not being able to get there. Serena was obviously stuck somewhere she didn't want to be, pining for Dan, wishing she were with him. Maybe she was on a subway somewhere, stuck between stops. And he was stuck in the park with Zeke.

"Hey," Dan said, shoving his notebook into his bag and standing up. "Thanks for showing up."

"Fuck you. I had math tutoring, you know that," Zeke said, dribbling the ball.

They headed toward the basketball court. "Yeah, well, you should work harder in math," Dan said. "Then you wouldn't need a tutor."

"And you should go fuck yourself, because you're lame," Zeke said.

"What's that's supposed to mean?" Dan asked. He dropped his bag by the court fence and peeled off his coat.

Zeke danced around with the ball. He was a little overweight and had wide hips like a girl, but he was the best basketball player at Riverside Prep. Go figure. "You're always busy these days, and you're always in a bad mood," he said. "You're getting lamer and lamer."

Dan shrugged and lunged forward to steal the ball away from Zeke. "Hey, what can I say? I have a girlfriend," he said, backing away and dribbling the ball down the court. He did a layup, missing the basket by a foot.

"Nice one, loser." Zeke sprinted up and caught the rebound. "A girlfriend?" he said, bouncing the ball without going anywhere. His belly jiggled beneath his white T-shirt. "Who, Vanessa?"

Dan shook his head. "Her name's Serena. You don't know her," he said. "We're going college visiting together this weekend."

"Wow," Zeke said, spinning around to dribble the ball down to the other basket. He didn't sound all that impressed.

Dan watched his friend take a perfect jump shot. He stood still as Zeke dribbled the ball back down the court.

"So, it's pretty serious, huh?" Zeke said, tossing him the ball.

Dan caught the ball and stayed where he was. He wasn't sure what to say to that. It was pretty serious to him, that was for sure. But was Serena at that very moment telling her friends all about Dan, her new boyfriend? Was she daydreaming about their weekend away together?

Not quite.

At that very moment, Serena was at the dentist, getting a cavity filled. She was hungry and a little pissed off that she was going to have to wait for the novocaine to wear off before she could eat anything.

Not exactly the stuff of poetry.

She had also read Dan's poem, and she wasn't sure what to do about it. She was used to guys' attention, but not this sort of attention. Dan was becoming vaguely stalkeresque, and it was really starting to weird her out.

b gets a new brother

"What sorts of questions have you prepared?" Ms. Glos asked Blair. It was Wednesday afternoon, and Ms. Glos was prepping Blair for her Yale interview on Saturday. "You'll need to show them that you're interested in things that are particular to Yale, that you're not just applying there because it's a good school and you're a legacy child."

Blair nodded impatiently. What did Ms. Glos think she was, a moron?

Ms. Glos uncrossed her legs and picked at a piece of lint stuck to her tan pantyhose. Her upper body was thick and square like a man's, but Blair noticed she had remarkably good legs for a fifty-year-old college advisor.

"I'm going to ask them about opportunities to travel in France junior year. I'm going to ask about their sports facilities and about housing. I'm going to ask about opportunities to participate in student government. Oh, and I'm going to ask about job recruitment," Blair said. She opened her PalmPilot and made a note to herself.

"Good girl. That will show that you're not just an academic. You're well-rounded, you're interested in participating." Ms. Glos closed Blair's file and slipped it back into a drawer in her desk. "You'll do fine," she told Blair. "You're more than ready."

Blair stood up. She already knew she was ready. She'd been prepping for this her whole life. "Thanks, Ms. Glos," she said and reached for the doorknob. "If it goes well, I can apply early and forget about looking at other schools, right?"

"Well, it can't hurt to look at a few other places—you might find somewhere else you like better," Ms. Glos said, dabbing at her nose with a Kleenex. "But I don't see why Yale wouldn't take you."

Blair smiled. "Good." Then she opened the door and closed it behind her, satisfied.

When Blair got home to the penthouse on Seventy-second Street, she could tell immediately that something was different. Suitcases and boxes littered the hallway. *TRL* was blaring from the giant TV in the library. She could hear the scratching of a dog's claws on the wood floors, and there was a leash hanging from the doorknob.

Blair walked inside and dropped her backpack on the floor of the foyer. She was greeted by an enormous brown boxer, who trotted up and butted his head into her crotch.

"Hey," she said, batting the dog's nose away. "Fuck off." She peered down the apartment's long hallway. "Mom?"

The door to her mother's bedroom opened and Cyrus Rose came out, wearing his favorite red silk Versace bathrobe and bamboo spa sandals. He looked very relaxed. "Hello, Blair!" he shouted, shuffling up and wrapping his arms around her in a bear hug. "Your mother's in the tub. But it's official—I'm all moved in. And Aaron and Mookie have moved in, too!"

"Mookie?" Blair said, stepping backward. She didn't like

standing so close to Cyrus when it was very possible he wasn't wearing anything under his bathrobe.

"Aaron's dog! He's a real mooch. Ha ha! Mookie the mooch," Cyrus said, snapping stubby, gold-ringed fingers. "Aaron's mom's away a whole lot, and he was bored as hell up in that big house in Scarsdale with only Mookie to talk to, so he decided to move in with us. Like your mom says, the more the merrier!"

Blair just stood there, unable to believe her ears. The dog, Mookie, walked up behind her and sniffed her butt.

"Mookie, no!" Cyrus said, laughing. "Come here, boy. Come help me introduce Blair to Aaron. Come on." He grabbed the dog's collar and led him into the library.

Blair had a feeling she was supposed to follow them, but she stood where she was, still in shock.

A moment later a head full of short brown dreadlocks darted out from behind the library door. The head belonged to a boy Blair's age, with big brown eyes, pale skin, and red lips that curved up at the corners.

"Hey," the boy said, "I'm Aaron." He tromped down the hallway in his work boots to offer Blair his hand. His T-shirt was ripped and had a faded picture of Bob Marley on it. Blair could see the tops of his underwear above the waistband of his baggy pants.

Ew?

Blair touched his hand as little as possible before pulling away.

"So I guess we're roommates now, huh?" Aaron said, still smiling.

Seriously ew.

"I hope you don't mind, but I shut your cat in your bedroom 'cause she was kind of freaked out by Mookie. Her tail got huge," he said and laughed, shaking his dreadlocks.

Blair glared at him. "I have to do my homework," she said and turned for her bedroom, slamming the door in Aaron's face.

Alone in her room, she grabbed the cat and threw herself onto her bed. Kitty Minky kneaded his paws into her sweater.

"It's okay, baby," Blair murmured, clutching him to her chest. She closed her eyes tight and burrowed her head into his soft fur, wishing the world would go away.

She kept her eyes closed and her body still. If she stayed like that for long enough, maybe everyone would forget about her and she wouldn't have to go on being Blair Waldorf, living her increasingly stupid life. She could become someone else and still go to Yale. Eventually, after searching and searching for years without giving up, Nate would find her. It would be like an old black-and-white movie where the heroine gets amnesia and starts a new life and falls in love with a new man, but all along the man who loved her originally never gave up searching until he found her and asked her to marry him, even though she couldn't remember his name. Then, when he gave her an old scarf of his, full of smells and old times together, her memory would come back and she'd say, "I do," and they'd live happily ever after.

The film credits rolled in her mind as violins played softly.

When all else failed, Blair could always go to the movies in her head. Best not tell the Yale admissions office that, though. They might give her a *p* for psychotic.

Finally Blair let go of Kitty Minky and sat up. She grabbed the remote for her TV and pressed play. The VCR whirred, and soon the opening scene of *Breakfast at Tiffany's* began playing over and over—Audrey Hepburn, still dressed up after a long night out, eating croissants in front of Tiffany's at daybreak. This was the film Blair had entered in the Constance

Billard film festival. Audrey eating croissants to the theme from *The Sorcerer's Apprentice,* admiring the diamonds in a Tiffany's window. And again, to an old Duran Duran song— "Girls on Film." Then again, to Liz Phair's "Rocketboy." And again to different music. Blair saw something different in the scene every time. She never got tired of it. Hopefully the judges at the festival next Monday would feel the same way.

There was a knock on the door, and Blair rolled over to see who could possibly have the nerve to disturb her. The door swung open. It was Aaron. Mookie nosed his way between his legs and into the room. Kitty Minky yowled and darted into the closet.

"Mookie, no!" Aaron growled, grabbing the dog's collar. "Sorry," he said, glancing apologetically at Blair. He pulled Mookie out the door and swatted his behind. "Bad," he scolded.

Blair just stared at him, chin in her hands, hating him more each second.

"Listen," Aaron said. "You want a beer or something?"

Blair didn't reply. She hated beer.

Aaron's dark brown eyes roamed to the TV screen. "Hey, you dig that old shit?" he said.

Blair grabbed the remote and clicked off the TV. No way was she going to allow Aaron to insult her film. Hadn't he done enough harm already?

"I know it must be pretty freaky for you with us moving in all of a sudden, and the wedding and everything. I just thought if you wanted to like, talk or whatever, that's cool," Aaron said.

Blair continued to stare at him coldly, wishing he'd get lost.

Aaron cleared his throat. "I was just hanging with your little brother Tyler, you know, like watching TV and drinking a beer. Well, I drank a beer—he had a Coke. Anyway, he seems pretty cool with the whole thing. He's a neat little kid."

Blair blinked. Did this asshole think they were having a conversation?

"Okay," Aaron said. "Um, we're all going out to dinner later. I'm vegan, so we're going to a vegetarian restaurant. Hope that's okay." He backed away, waited for a moment for Blair to respond. When she didn't, he smiled resignedly and closed the door.

Blair rolled over again and hugged a pillow against her stomach. Of course he was vegan. It was so typical. She wished she had some raw meat to throw in his face.

What? Did everyone expect her to give her new faux-hip-pie stepbrother a warm welcome just because he was living in the house, drinking beer like he owned the place, and hanging out with Tyler like Mr. Sensitive? Well, they could take that idea and shove it up their fat asses.

At least she was getting away this weekend, and pretty soon she'd be at Yale and away from this freak show forever. Maybe if she told Nate what had happened, he would feel sorry for her and decide to come with her to New Haven after all.

She reached for the phone beside her bed and dialed Nate's number.

"Yo," Nate answered it on the fifth ring. He sounded baked.

"Hey, it's me," Blair said, her voice trembling a little. All of a sudden she felt like she might cry.

"Hey."

Blair rolled onto her back and stared up at the ceiling. Kitty Minky peered out of the closet, her eyes glowing yellow. "Um, I was wondering if maybe you changed your mind and wanted to come up to Yale with me— " Blair's voice broke off. She really was going to cry.

"Nah, the guys are all psyched for our road trip," Nate said.

"Okay," Blair said. "I just . . . this whole wedding thing . . .

and now . . ." She stopped. Tears fell out of the corners of her eyes and ran down her cheeks.

"Hey, are you crying?" Nate asked.

Fresh tears fell out of Blair's eyes. Nate sounded like he was thousands of miles away. She was too upset to explain everything to him. He hadn't even thanked her for her present. *What the fuck?*

"I have to go," Blair sniffed. "Call me tomorrow, okay?"

"I will," Nate said. But Blair could already tell that he wouldn't. He probably wouldn't even remember the phone call. He was too baked.

"'Bye," Blair said and clicked off. She tossed the phone on her bed and scratched her nails against the bedspread. Kitty Minky crept out of the closet and jumped up on the bed.

"It's okay, baby," Blair told her, stroking her head. She picked the cat up and put her on her stomach. "It's okay."

Kitty Minky closed her eyes and settled into the warm folds of her sweater, purring contentedly. Blair wished she could find someone to make her feel that content. She'd thought Nate was that someone, but he was turning out to be just as crappy and disappointing as everything else in her messed up life.

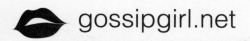 gossipgirl.net

Disclaimer: All the real names of places, people, and events have been altered or abbreviated to protect the innocent. Namely, me.

hey people!

FAMILY MATTERS

I know hate is a strong word and everything, but it's okay: we're teenagers. We're supposed to hate our parents every once in a while. We're also allowed to hate any siblings, older or younger, who annoy us, especially those not even related to us who we didn't even ask for.

However, if one of these unasked for siblings happens to be a rather cute boy with dreadlocks who I happen to know is a very good guitar player and is just about the sweetest boy in the entire world, you might want to be nice. Innocent flirting with your stepbrother-to-be isn't sick or illegal. In fact, it's pretty fun and pretty damned convenient if you live in the same house! It's just a thought. Although it doesn't look like **B** has considered this option.

Your E-Mail

 Dear Gossip Girl,
I hear **B** is a total klepto. Like in kindergarten she stole other kids' Barbie erasers and pencils and shit. And you couldn't invite her over for sleepovers cause she'd steal your clothes. I also heard she stole a watch from Tiffany.
—Peekaboo

 Dear Peekaboo,
B's been wearing a Rolex since sophomore year so I'm not sure about that one. Thanks for the scoop, tho.
—GG

Q: hey gossip grl,
i'm pretty sure i saw n talking to that constance ninth grader
outside the gap on 86th Street.
—owl99

 A: Dear owl99,
And?? They're already old news. You're going to have to do
better than that.
—GG

Sightings

N buying a super-family-sized bag of pot at his trusty pizza place on the corner of Eightieth and Madison. Preparing for his road trip, I guess. *B* and her new and enlarged family in **Saks,** shopping merrily for wedding things. Actually, *B* spent most of her time there in the ladies lounge, sulking. *S* wandering through the cosmetics department of **Barneys** again, biting her nails. *D* pining on a bench in **Riverside Park,** chain-smoking. *J* scribbling *N*'s name in discreet places all over town using her excellent calligraphy. My placemat at **Jackson Hole** was covered with it.

COLLEGE VISITING MUST-HAVES

A car.

Friends. Preferably ones who aren't so hyped up about college that they're going to freak out if you decide to skip the college tour and watch movies and play drinking games in the motel room instead.

Clothes you don't mind sleeping in and leaving behind in the motel rooms you're probably going to trash en route.

Nice clothes to wear to your interview. You don't want to look too fabulous, though, or you might give your interviewer an inferiority complex. Most of them don't know the difference between **Barneys** and Wal-Mart.

Sundries (Bud in cans, Entenmann's chocolate-covered donuts, Pringles, etc.).

You know you love me,

gossip girl

b gets the hell out

"You don't think it's too Little Bo Peep?" Blair's mother asked. She twirled around on the raised platform in Saks Fifth Avenue's bridal department, the skirt of the white satin-and-lace wedding dress fanning out around her feet.

Blair shook her head. The sight of her mother all dolled up in a pouffy white low-cut wedding dress made her want to gag, but the sooner they were out of there the better. She had to get ready for her Yale interview tomorrow. "It looks nice," she lied.

"It's kind of shameful for me to wear white," Mrs. Waldorf mused. "I mean, I already had my white wedding." She turned to Blair. "What if I had it dyed? It might look lovely in a nice golden beige or a pale lilac."

Blair shrugged and shifted uncomfortably on the fake antique loveseat she was sitting on. "I don't mind white." The dyeing thing sounded like it would take longer.

"We can always dye it once it's made," the saleswoman suggested. "Shall I go ahead and fit you for this one, then?" Even she was getting impatient. They had already been through seven dresses and three skirt-and-jacket combinations. If Mrs. Waldorf wanted her dress to be ready in only two weeks, she was going to have to hurry her ass up.

Blair's mother stopped twirling and examined herself critically in the four-way mirror. "I do think it's the most flattering one I've tried on," she said. "Don't you, Blair?"

Blair nodded enthusiastically. "Definitely, Mom. It makes you look tiny."

Her mother smiled, delighted.

The way to any girl's heart is to tell her she looks tiny. Girls kill to be tiny.

"All right then," she said, glowing with excitement. "Let's do it."

The saleswoman began tucking and pinning the dress, measuring things and jotting them down on a piece of paper. Blair looked at her watch. It was already three-thirty. This whole boring episode was taking *for-fucking-ever*.

"Have you found anything you like for the bridesmaids to wear?" her mother called over to her.

"Not yet," Blair said, although she hadn't even looked. Her mother wanted her to find one off-the-rack dress that she absolutely loved and get it for all the bridesmaids. Blair loved to shop, but she was having a hard time getting excited about buying this particular dress. She hated wearing the same thing as other people. After all, she'd spent most of her life in a fucking school uniform.

"I saw a gorgeous one in Barneys. Chloé, I think the designer was. Chocolate beaded silk with spaghetti straps. Long, cut on the bias. Very sophisticated. It would look stunning on Serena, with her slim legs and fair coloring. I'm not sure though—it might make you look a little . . . hippy."

Blair glared at her mother's reflection in the mirror in stunned silence. Was she suggesting that Blair was *fat*? Fatter than Serena?

Blair stood up and picked up her book bag. "I'm going

home, Mom," she said angrily. "I don't have time to talk about clothes anymore. In case you'd forgotten, I have my Yale interview tomorrow, which, to me, is kind of more important."

Her mother whirled around, causing the saleswoman to drop her pincushion. "That reminds me!" Mrs. Waldorf cried, completely oblivious to Blair's hurt tone of voice. "When Cyrus heard you were planning to take the train up to New Haven tomorrow, he had a terrific brainstorm."

Uh-oh.

Any brainstorm of Cyrus's had to be hellish. Blair cocked her head, preparing for the worst.

"It's all arranged—Aaron's going to take you! He wants to look at Yale, too, and he has a car parked in a garage on Lexington," her mother explained in a rush. "Isn't that just *perfect?*"

Blair felt like she was going to cry again. *No!* she wanted to shout. *It isn't perfect, Mom! It sucks!* But she wasn't about to cry in the bridal department at Saks. That would be beyond pathetic.

"I'll see you later," she said abruptly, turning to leave.

Her mother frowned after her. *Poor Blair,* she thought. *She must be nervous about her Yale interview.*

Blair walked the twenty-two blocks home biting back tears of outrage. She thought about checking into the Pierre Hotel and beginning the first stages of her disappearance. She could call her father and ask to live with him and his boyfriend in their château in France. She could learn how to stomp grapes, or whatever the hell they did there.

But she had to finish her senior year at Constance. She had to finally do it with Nate. And she had to go to Yale.

She was going to have to suck it up.

When she got upstairs to the penthouse, Mookie dashed down the hallway and hurled himself at her, licking her face and wriggling his bottom exuberantly. Blair dropped her book bag and sat on the floor, letting the dog tread all over her as the tears rolled down her cheeks. Mookie's breath smelled like ass.

She'd definitely hit an all-time low.

Aaron poked his head out of the library. "Hey, what's up?" he asked, walking over to her. "Mookie, no!" he yelled, pulling the dog away. "You shouldn't let him do that. He's going to fall in love with you and starting humping your leg and stuff."

Blair stifled a sob and wiped her nose with the back of her hand.

"So, you ready to rock on up to Yale tomorrow?" Aaron asked, holding out his hand to pull her up off the floor.

Blair ignored his hand. She wanted a drink badly. "I can't wait to get the hell out of here," she mumbled miserably.

"Well, we could leave now if you want. It'd be more fun if we didn't have to wake up early to get you up there for your interview," Aaron said. He pushed his dreadlocks behind his ears. Blair had never seen anyone do that before.

"Now?" Blair accepted Aaron's hand and stood up shakily. It wasn't what she'd planned. But why the hell not? This way, she and Aaron would be on the road at night. They'd have to stay in a hotel somewhere. They'd have a car. They could go anywhere. Anywhere that wasn't here.

She was going to be spontaneous for once.

"Okay," Blair said with a sniffle. "I just have to pack."

"Cool," Aaron said. "Me too. Hey Tyler!" he shouted. Tyler padded out of the library in his sock feet. He was wearing one of Aaron's Legalize Hemp T-shirts and had chocolate on his face. "Sorry, man, I can't finish watching *The Matrix* sequel with you," Aaron told him. "Blair and I are going on a road trip."

"That's cool," Tyler said. "Sequels suck."

Blair pushed past her brother and hurried into her bedroom to get ready. Her heart was pounding. She might have hated Aaron, but she was so eager to get the fuck out of there she didn't even mind that it had to be with him. Just as long as he didn't try to act all brotherly and Mother Naturey and shit.

rendezvous at grand central station

When Serena arrived at the bar upstairs in Grand Central Station, Dan was already there, smoking a cigarette and drinking a gin and tonic. He looked nervous.

"Hey," Serena said breathlessly.

She was always breathless because she was always late. Dan liked to imagine her descending from the heavens to get there. It was a long flight.

"Our cook gave me some sandwiches in case we get hungry," she said.

Her cook! Well, she *was* a fairy princess—of course she had a cook.

Dan swirled the ice around in his glass. Serena was wearing a blue sweater that made her eyes look bigger and bluer than he had ever seen them.

"I brought a bottle of wine," he told her. "We can have a picnic."

Serena slid onto the bar stool next to him. The bartender placed a Kir royale, all bubbly and lavender-colored, on the cocktail napkin in front of her. "I love this place," she said, picking up the drink.

The bartender already knew what she wanted. How cool was that?

Dan offered her a cigarette, put one in his mouth, and lit them both. He felt incredibly suave.

Serena exhaled, blowing smoke at the station's ornate ceiling. "I think the thing I love most about going someplace is the stations and the airports and the taxis. They're so . . . sexy," she said.

Dan sucked on his cigarette. "Yeah," he said, although he couldn't have disagreed more. He couldn't wait to just *get there*. As soon as he and Serena were alone he would . . .

Yes?

He wasn't sure what was going to happen, but he was sure it was going to be something.

"You'll like my brother, Erik," Serena said, sipping the Kir royale. "He likes to philosophize. But he's kind of a big partier, too."

Dan nodded and pulled at his brown curls. He'd forgotten about Erik. Hopefully Erik would be partying with his roommates while they were there. That way Dan would have Serena all to himself.

The departures and arrivals boards flashed and fluttered as new times were posted and trains came and went. The station was busy with the weekend rush. People dashed to meet their trains or stood around waiting to greet their friends.

Serena squinted at the departures board. "Our train leaves in fifteen minutes," she said. "One more cigarette for the road, and then we should go."

Dan fished two more cigarettes out of the pack and swiveled around on his stool to pick up his lighter.

"So," Serena said. "I read your poem." She had to bring it up sometime, and now was as good as ever. The poem was good, but it still freaked her out.

Dan froze.

Out of the corner of his eye, he saw four vaguely familiar boys saunter into the Vanderbilt Avenue entrance to the station. One of them stopped and stared at Serena.

Nate was baked, but he wasn't hallucinating. Serena van der Woodsen was sitting right there at the Grand Central bar, wearing white flared cords, a bright blue V-neck sweater, and her favorite pair of brown suede boots. The sweater made her eyes look deeper and darker than he'd ever seen them.

Blair had made him promise to forget about Serena, but Nate had never been sure if he'd succeeded. He'd been trying to avoid her, because seeing Serena usually made his heart hurt.

Not this time, though. This time, something was different. When he looked at Serena all he saw was a beautiful old friend.

"Hey, I know those boys!" Serena said, hopping off her stool. She left her unlit cigarette on the bar and walked over to Nate.

"Wait," Dan said. She hadn't told him what she thought of his poem.

He watched Serena approach the boy who'd been staring at her and kiss him on the cheek. All of a sudden Dan knew why these boys looked so familiar. They were the same boys he'd seen playing ball with his sister in the park.

"Hey, guys," Serena said, smiling her inimitable smile. "Where're you going?"

It was just like her to walk up, give Nate a kiss, and say "Hey," as if she hadn't noticed that Nate had been ignoring her ever since she'd come back to New York last month.

Serena wasn't one to hold a grudge. Unlike some people we know.

"We're heading up to Brown," Anthony said. "But first we have to pick up Jeremy's mom's car in New Canaan."

Serena's eyes lit up. "No way. We're going up to Brown, too! My brother goes there, so we're staying with him. Want to ride with us?"

Nate frowned. Riding up to Brown with Serena was definitely not in Blair's you-can-go-away-without-me rule book. But who said he had to follow *her* rules?

"Right on," said Jeremy. "Sounds like a party."

"Cool," Serena said. "You guys can probably stay with my brother, too." She turned and waved at the pale scruffy boy hunched over the bar. "Hey, Dan. Come here."

Dan got up and came over. Serena noticed he looked a little sad.

"Guys, this is Dan. Dan this is Nate, Charlie, Jeremy, and Anthony. They're going to ride with us up to Brown."

Serena smiled brightly at Dan, and he tried to smile back—he really did, but it was hard. Why hadn't they gotten on the train early? They could've been happily drinking wine and eating Serena's cook's sandwiches instead of sharing rides with four spoiled St. Jude's boys who would totally monopolize Serena and change the whole tone of the trip. There would be no whispering to each other in all-night diners, holding hands under the table. No sleeping together on her brother's floor. It wasn't a romantic weekend away anymore: it was a college-visiting road trip, a meaningless party.

Woo-hoo!

Dan had never felt so disappointed. "Cool," he said. He wished he were back in his room, writing about the weekend that could have been.

"Okay, let's roll. We better make that train," Charlie said.

Serena slipped her arm through Dan's and pulled him down the steps with her. "Come on!" she cried, running.

Dan stumbled after her. He had no choice.

Nate walked behind them, feeling a little bit sad himself. He wished he'd brought someone with him, and it wasn't Blair he was thinking of.

best western vs. motel 6

"Maybe we should drive through Middletown on the way. Look at Wesleyan," Aaron suggested. He punched in the Saab's lighter and opened the sunroof.

They had just pulled onto I-95 in Connecticut. Blair had ridden the whole way in silence as Aaron maneuvered his way out of the city. Some kind of hippie-happy reggae music she had never heard of was playing on the stereo.

"You want to lively up yourself!"

Blair slipped off her shoes and put her sock feet up on the dashboard. "I'm not applying anywhere else but Yale," she said. "But we can drive through Wesleyan if you want."

Aaron pulled a cigarette out of a funny-looking tin and lit it. He cocked his head at Blair. "What makes you so sure you're getting in?" he asked.

Blair shrugged. "I've been planning to go there since I was little," she said in explanation. "Is that pot?"

"No way, man," Aaron said with a grin. "They're herbal. Want to try one?"

Blair made a face and pulled a pack of Merit Ultra Lights out of her bag. "I prefer these," she said.

"Those things will kill you," Aaron remarked. He slipped

the car into the middle lane and took a deep drag. "These are one hundred percent natural."

Blair glared out the window. She really didn't feel like being lectured on the holistic qualities of Aaron's special cigarettes. "Thanks, but no thanks," she said, hoping that would put an end to the conversation.

"So I'm trying to figure out whether you're a big partier or not," Aaron said. "Something tells me that when you let your hair down, you can get pretty crazy."

Blair continued to stare out the window. Actually, he was right, but she really didn't give a crap what Aaron thought. Let him think what he wanted to think.

"Not really," she said, puffing her cigarette.

"So, do you have a boyfriend?"

"Yes."

"But he doesn't want to go to Yale?"

"No. I mean, he does," Blair corrected, "but he's looking at Brown this weekend. He's going up there with a few friends."

Aaron nodded. "I see," he said.

Something about the way he said it completely infuriated Blair. It was like he saw right through her and Nate and knew that she had practically gotten down on her hands and knees and begged Nate to come up to New Haven with her, but he'd refused.

Aaron could go fuck himself for making her feel like shit.

"Look, it's really none of your business," Blair snapped. "Let's just get there, okay?"

Aaron shook his head and pointed at the tin of herbal cigarettes that he'd placed on the dash. "You sure you don't want one?" he asked. "They'll mellow you out."

Blair shook her head.

"Fine," Aaron said. He pulled out into the left lane and revved the engine up to ninety.

Blair glanced at his hand on the stick shift. His thumbnail was bruised a purpley-black color, and he was wearing a silver thumb ring in the shape of a snake. If he hadn't been her almost stepbrother, it would have been kind of sexy.

But he was, and it wasn't.

Dan was too depressed to even think about getting high with Nate's friends in the backseat. The whole way on the train up to Ridgefield, Serena and Nate and his friends had talked about stuff Dan didn't know about. Like bars he'd never heard of, or places in the country where he'd never been sailing or played tennis. Dan had spent last summer working part time at a bookstore on Broadway and part time at a deli. He got free books at the bookstore, and at the deli he got to drink as much coffee as he wanted. It was great. But he hadn't shared that little piece of trivia. It was anything but glamorous.

Dan knew Serena wasn't trying to be a snob. She wasn't like that. She didn't need to climb up the social ladder—she was already on the top rung. What depressed him was that she didn't want to be alone with him the way he wanted to be alone with her. If she did, she wouldn't have turned their cozy weekend away into a rockin' slumber party.

"Who wants one?" Serena called from the passenger seat. She turned and dangled a six-pack of Bud into the backseat.

"Me!" All four of the other boys cried out eagerly, including Nate, who was driving.

"No way, Nate," Serena said. "You have to wait till we stop."

"Aw, come on," Nate said. "I was baked when I took my driving test."

"Sorry," Serena told him, passing a beer back to Charlie. "You wanted to be Big Daddy the Driver. Now you have to pay."

Anthony giggled and kicked the back of Nate's seat. "Daddy, are we there yet?"

"Shut up back there," Nate shouted gruffly. "Or I'm going to have to pull over and spank the tar out of you."

The back seat erupted in laughter.

Dan sat hunched by the window, watching the billboards on I-95 flash by, hating Nate and his friends. First they'd taken his sister away and now his girlfriend. As if they didn't already have everything they could possibly want handed to them on a fucking silver platter. Dan knew that wasn't exactly fair, but he didn't feel like being fair. He was pissed.

He reached in his pocket for a Camel, his hands shaking more than ever.

One thing was certain. He wasn't on this trip for nothing. Tomorrow he was going to ace his fucking Brown interview.

Aaron saw a sign for a Motel 6 about twenty miles before New Haven and turned off the exit.

"What are you doing?" Blair said. "We're not there yet."

"Yeah, but it's a Motel 6. We're close enough," Aaron said, as if that explained everything.

"What's so great about Motel 6?"

"They're clean. They're cheap. They have cable. And their vending machines rock," Aaron said.

"I thought we were going to stay someplace nice, with room service," Blair said. She'd never been to a motel before.

"Trust me," Aaron said, pulling up outside the motel office.

Blair stayed in the car with her arms folded sullenly across her chest, while Aaron went in to register. He was trying to act all down with the people and pretend he wasn't a spoiled rich boy from the suburbs. It was so annoying. Still, she felt kind of seedy driving up to a motel in a red Saab with a boy with dreadlocks. The parking lot was dim and the rooms were all shaded with curtains. It looked like the kind of place people went to disappear from a previous life.

Aaron came back with one key. "They only had one room left. It's got a big bed, though. You okay with that?"

Blair was certain Aaron was expecting her to throw a hissy fit and demand her own room.

"Fine," she said. She could deal.

Aaron got back in the car and screeched out of the parking lot and back onto the main road.

"Where are we going now?" Blair demanded. She hated Aaron's way of just doing whatever the hell he pleased, never mind what she wanted.

"That's the other great thing about Motel 6es. They're always on roads with cheesy strip malls, so you can get everything you need," Aaron said. He turned into the parking lot of a Shop 'n' Save and pulled his mother's Shop 'n' Save credit card out of his wallet. "Come on, let's splurge," he said.

Blair rolled her eyes.

At least he knew how to use plastic.

Nate drove until he couldn't stand it anymore. His friends had been giggling in the back seat for two and a half hours, and he needed a beer.

"I'm pulling over," he said. "I saw a Best Western sign. They're okay, right?"

"My family stayed in a suite in a Best Western upstate when we were dropping my sister off at camp," Dan said. "It was nice."

"They have suites?" Jeremy said. "I thought Best Westerns were like, motels."

"It had room service," Dan said a little defensively. "And a fridge full of drinks."

"We're definitely getting a suite," Charlie said.

Dan closed his eyes and prayed that there weren't any suites in this particular Best Western. There was still hope that he and Serena might wind up sharing their own room together. It might be almost better than he'd hoped.

The bed in the Motel 6 was loaded with snack food. Chips Ahoy, Fritos, Wise potato chips, Smart Food, dairy-free chocolate pudding, Hawaiian Punch, soy Swiss cheese, Ritz crackers, and, of course, beer in cans.

"I bet there's something good on TNT," Aaron said, plunking himself down on the end of the bed. He cracked open a Bud and reached for another one of his special cigarettes.

Blair fluffed up a pillow and leaned against the headboard, tucking her knees neatly under her chin. She'd never done exactly this before—eaten crap and drunk Bud in a motel room with a boy she didn't know very well while watching bad TV. It was kind of . . . different.

"I'll have one of those," she said quietly.

Aaron kept his eyes on the TV and handed her a beer, his silver snake ring flashing. "See, I told you. *Die Hard 2*. Excellent."

"And one of those," Blair said, pointing to his cigarette.

Aaron turned and smiled crookedly at her out of the side of his mouth. "I'm telling you, they make you feel really mellow," he warned.

"Fine," Blair said evenly.

She'd had a stressful past few days. Why shouldn't she relax?

Aaron flipped her a cigarette and handed her a pack of matches. "Careful not to inhale too quick, or you'll fry your lungs."

Blair rolled her eyes, annoyed. She knew how to smoke. The

back of Aaron's T-shirt read POWER TO THE PEOPLE, which also annoyed her. He thought he was so cool and liberal and politically aware. She lit a match and held it up to the cigarette. Just a quick smoke, a few sips of beer, and maybe a donut, and then she was going to bed early.

Tomorrow she had her future to contend with.

The Best Western suite had two double beds and a pull-out sofa. There were hunting scenes on the walls, and through the large, rectangular window was a view of a local fairgrounds, closed for the winter. The Ferris wheel hovered in the night air like an obese skeleton. Dan couldn't stop staring at it.

Nate and his friends had ordered a bunch of pizzas and a case of beer and were lying all over the beds fighting over the remote. Jeremy wanted to watch pornos on pay-per-view. Nate wanted to watch an old spaghetti western on Bravo. Charlie wanted to turn out all the lights and open all the windows and listen to Radiohead on the CD player.

Serena was taking a shower. Dan could smell the steam from underneath the bathroom door. It smelled like lavender and candle wax. Serena was singing.

"Voulez vous couchez avec moi, ce soir?"

Yes, Dan did want to sleep with her tonight. Badly. But it didn't look like that was going to happen.

"Hey, you boys better not be getting pepperoni grease on my bed," Serena warned, opening the bathroom door, her body wrapped in a big white hotel towel.

"Which one is your bed?" Anthony asked, burping loudly.

"I haven't decided yet," Serena replied. "But if you're going to burp and fart all over that one, maybe I'll sleep on the other one."

She walked across the room to her bag and pulled a gray sweatshirt and a pair of plaid flannel boxers out of it.

Every one of the boys watched her. It was kind of hard not to.

"And don't eat all the pizza, either," Serena said, marching back to the bathroom to change. "I'm starving."

Dan lit a cigarette, his hands shaking harder than ever. He got up from his chair by the window, grabbed a beer off the bed, and sat down on the sofa. He had nothing better to do. He might as well get drunk.

Serena came back out of the bathroom wearing the sweatshirt and boxers. She picked up a can of beer and a slice of pizza and sat down on the sofa next to Dan. It was such a relief to have the other three boys along for the trip. The poem Dan had sent her had been all about love and death and how he wanted to keep on living because of her. Serena liked Dan a lot, but he really needed to lighten up.

"Here's to college," she said, slapping her pizza against Dan's beer can. "Wouldn't it be funny if we all wound up going to Brown together?"

Dan nodded, threw his beer back, and stood up for another one. *Yeah, that'd be funny all right,* he thought. *Hilarious.*

Blair lay back on the bed and held a Ritz cracker over her left eye, squinting at the ceiling with her right one. A tiny spider walked toward the overhead light.

"Gross. There's a spider on the ceiling," she told Aaron. She had drunk three beers and eaten four donuts. She was having Ritz crackers and spray-on cheddar cheese for dessert.

"Know what we forgot?" Aaron said, kicking the empty beer cans off the bed and shoving a handful of Fritos in his mouth.

"Water?" Blair said. She had eaten so much sugar, salt, and grease she was dying of thirst.

The three herbal cigarettes she'd smoked hadn't helped either.

"No," Aaron said. "Candy."

Blair smiled. A KitKat might be nice.

"Okay," she said.

They tiptoed out of their room and down the hall to the vending machine. Blair burst out laughing when she saw the hall carpet. It was brown with red swirls. Who decorated these places, anyway?

Aaron stood in front of the vending machine, frowning. "I can't decide," he said.

Blair stood next to him. They had KitKats, but they also had Twixes and Snickers and Almond Joys. It was a tough decision.

"How much change do we have?" she asked seriously.

Aaron held out his hand. They had enough for exactly two and a half candy bars. Or two candy bars and some gum.

Blair burst out laughing again. "I'm getting straight A's in AP calculus, and I can't even pick out a fucking candy bar," she said.

Aaron took three quarters and dropped them into the slot. Then he grabbed her hand. "Okay, close your eyes and pick one."

He guided her hand toward the machine until her fingers were just skimming the buttons. Blair pressed her finger on the button and heard something drop into the bottom of the machine. She bent down to pick it up.

"Wait!" Aaron cried, pulling her back. "Let's do another one and then see what we got." He dropped another three quarters into the slot.

Blair tried to remember where the KitKats had been, but

she couldn't. She pressed another button, and again something dropped to the bottom of the machine. Blair opened her eyes and rushed forward to retrieve their booty. An Almond Joy and a pack of Lifesavers.

"Lifesavers? No way!" she cried.

"Way!" Aaron said, grabbing the Almond Joy out of her hand and racing down the hallway.

"Wait, that's mine!" Blair yelled and tore after him, slipping on the thin carpet in her sock feet. It was just after two o'clock in the morning. Her interview was in less than nine hours, and she hated to admit it, but she was actually having kind of a good time.

Yale, schmale.

Dan lay on the sofa bed, listening to Charlie snoring softly beside him. Across the room Serena was sleeping in one of the double beds with Anthony, or was it Nate? He couldn't tell. Her mouth hung open on the pillow, and he could see her front teeth glistening in the moonlight. Outside, the Ferris wheel loomed like a giant eye, watching them. Dan rolled over to face the wall. He wanted to get up and write a poem, but he'd left his notebook behind. He'd thought he'd be too busy enjoying himself with Serena to want to write anything serious this weekend. He was just beginning to learn that nothing ever turns out the way you think it's going to.

Life sucks and then you die. Maybe that was what Sartre had really been trying to say in *No Exit*.

Dan threw off the covers and stood up. On his way to the bathroom to get a glass of water, he walked past the bed where Serena and Nate were sleeping. It was definitely Nate—he could see that now. And on the pillow between them were their hands . . . clasped tightly together.

They were holding hands in their sleep.

Dan turned away, picked up a pen off the bedside table, and locked himself in the bathroom.

When you have the uncontrollable urge to write a heart-wrenching poem about the absurdity of human existence, toilet paper will always do in a pinch.

Blair knew she was sleeping funny. The bag of Chips Ahoy was very close to her face and she was still wearing her bra, but she'd deal with that in the morning. Her stomach felt full and warm, and she really should have tried to make herself throw up if she wanted to keep fitting into her favorite pair of leather pants, but that, too, could wait until morning. Next to her, Aaron was laughing in his sleep and clapping his hands together, as if he were trying to call his dog. *Woofie?* Was that his dog's name? Blair thought hard, but she couldn't remember. She couldn't even remember why she was there, in a strange motel room with Aaron and his dreadlocks. But it was nice to fall asleep to the scent of chocolate chip cookies and the piney smoke of his one hundred percent natural cigarettes. It reminded her of Nate.

Hmm. Sounds like someone finally let her hair down. Sounds like someone also forgot to ask the motel reception desk for a wake-up call.

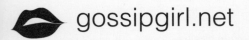

gossipgirl.net

topics ◄ *previous* **next** ► *post a question* *reply*

Disclaimer: All the real names of places, people, and events have been altered or abbreviated to protect the innocent. Namely, me.

hey people!

THE LEFT-BEHINDS

Okay, where the hell is everybody? Should I feel like a total loser for staying in the city this weekend? I did all my college visiting this summer—okay so I am a loser. Anyway, I pretty much know which ones are cool and which ones aren't, and what I don't know I can get from the catalogs. The only reason for me to visit a school now is to party with the people there, and frankly, I think we have the highest GPA in partying right here in good old NYC.

Anyway, everybody may be out of town, but we haven't lost touch. Check out the e-mails I've been getting.

Your e-mail:

 yo gossip girl,
i work at the motel 6 outside the town of orange in connecticut. so this 2 cute boy in this sweet red saab with new york plates pulls up, right? so of course i have to see who's with him. the girl looked pretty bitchy, to be honest, and totally not his type. anyway, i got off work and went home, but i know they were definitely partying in their room like, all night, because the whole hallway stank of weird smoke. the light was on in their car when i left. i hope they turned it off or the battery is going to be dead today.
—kiera3

 Dear kiera3,
Oops, sounds like **B** is in for a tough morning.
—GG

Q: Hey Gossip Girl,

I went up to Yale on Friday, too, and I am staying at the Motel 6. Okay. I know **B** and her stepbrother are like, almost related and everything. But I swear I saw them fooling around in the parking lot. Is that gross or what?
—MsPink

A: Dear MsPink,

I want to not believe you because yeah, that is gross.
—GG

Q: Dear Gossip Girl,

I heard that the cops showed up at a Best Western somewhere in Mass. and busted up a party full of kids. Apparently everyone involved spent the night in jail. Just thought you'd want to know.
—Dragonfly

A: Dear Dragonfly,

I don't know if our friends are dumb enough to get busted or not. I hope not!
—GG

Sightings

Let's stick to the city, shall we? **J** moping in **Central Park** Friday after school. Guess she misses **N** terribly. **V** putting the finishing touches on her movie. She's hosting a preview at **The Five and Dime** this weekend. Pretty cocky of her, if you ask me. **D** buying new razors at a drugstore on Forty-second Street before heading into **Grand Central Station** on Friday. Guess he wanted to be nice and clean shaven for **S**. **A** buying a cheesy Hallmark card in CVS on Friday on his way to get the car. Wonder who it was for?

That's all for now. I'm sure there'll be lots more news when everyone gets back.

Keep up the good work.

You know you love me,

gossip girl

the morning after

Sunshine streamed through the window, hitting the bag of Chips Ahoy hard enough to melt the chips. Blair caught the scent of gooey chocolate and woke up. She rolled over, knocking into Aaron, and then rolled the other way, crushing the half-empty bag of Fritos.

"Shit," she muttered under her breath. She pulled her watch up close to her face and stared at it. Her Yale interview was at eleven. She was lying facedown on a bag of Fritos in a seedy motel room in East Asshole, Connecticut, and it was already *ten o'clock.*

"Fuck!" Blair cried, leaping out of bed. "Aaron. Wake up. Now!"

It was kind of hard not to note the panic in her voice. "What time is it?" Aaron mumbled. He sat up, shaking his head back and forth sleepily.

"Three minutes after ten!" Blair screeched at him, digging through her bag. She hadn't even bothered to hang up her clothes, so her interview skirt was all rumpled. What was wrong with her? Was this not, like, the most important day of her life?

"Don't worry," Aaron said.

It was the wrong thing to say.

"*Shut up!*" Blair screamed, throwing a black Gucci loafer at him. "This is all your fault!"

Aaron reached under the covers to scratch his butt. "What's my fault?"

"Just shut up," Blair said. She wadded up her clothes, stomped into the bathroom, and slammed the door.

"I'm going to go see if they have coffee by the front desk," Aaron called out to her. "I'll check us out and wait for you by the car."

He swung his feet to the floor and pulled his jeans on. Then he stood up and examined his reflection in the motel room mirror. One dreadlock stuck straight up from the middle of his head. There was a chocolate smudge on his T-shirt. Aaron shrugged. He wasn't the one having the interview. He pulled his jacket on and grabbed the room key. No way was Blair going to blame him for screwing her life up. He'd get her there.

In the shower, Blair scrubbed at herself furiously as she went over practice interview questions in her head.

Why Yale? Because it's the best. I'm not going to college to have fun. I want the best teachers and the best selection of courses offered and the best facilities. I don't want to just get through the next four years. I want to be challenged.

Tell me about yourself. What kind of person are you? I'm very organized (chuckle). My friends think I'm kind of anal. I'm ambitious. I can't stand the idea of being just average at anything. I'm determined. I push myself to do the best I can. I suppose I'm a little stubborn. I'm very social. I organize parties and charity events. I try to stay politically aware, although with all the reading at school, I have to admit I don't read the paper every day. I love animals. I try to be a thoughtful daughter and sister and do nice things for my family without them asking.

Who is your role model? I have two. Jacqueline Kennedy

Onassis and Audrey Hepburn. They were both remarkable, strong, respected, beautiful women. Full of grace.

Blair turned off the tap and grabbed a towel. She didn't have time to wash her hair. Hopefully it wouldn't reek of smoke. She examined her face in the mirror. Her eyes were puffy, and a small zit shone pinkly above her left eyebrow. She spritzed her face with cucumber toner and dabbed La Mer eye cream under her eyes. Yale wasn't admitting her based on her looks, anyway. She pulled on her light blue Calvin Klein button-down shirt, her black pleated DKNY skirt, and black tights. Then she brushed her hair back into a loose ponytail. There. She looked like the kind of girl who liked to hang out in bookstores reading poetry. She looked serious and intelligent.

Blair dug around in her cosmetics bag for her Stila compact. She brushed a light pink glow over her cheeks, the bridge of her nose, and her forehead. Then she smeared some clear gloss on her lips. She was as ready as she'd ever be.

Ignoring the sick, nervous feeling in the pit of her bloated stomach, Blair stuffed her things into her bag, slipped on her Gucci loafers and her black wool coat, and charged out of the room. She was organized, ambitious, determined, politically aware . . . she reached the bottom of the staircase and pushed open the door to the parking lot. The hood was up on the Saab. Aaron was bent over the engine, attaching some kind of clamp to the battery. Blair stopped and sucked in her breath. What the hell was wrong with the fucking car?

Aaron turned around and squinted at her. "Battery's dead," he said. "We must have left the lights on all night."

"*We?*" Blair dropped her bag and stamped her foot angrily. "Now what am I supposed to do?" she wailed.

"The manager's going to jump-start us," Aaron said, pushing his dreadlocks behind his ears. "It's cool."

"Excuse me, but it is *not cool*. We should be there by now!" Blair screamed, even though Aaron was standing right in front of her.

A bleached blond woman in her forties pulled up beside the Saab in an old brown Suburban. She left the motor running and hopped out.

"Let's get this done quick," she told Aaron. "I don't like to leave the phones ringing." She lifted up the hood of the Suburban.

Blair looked at her watch again. It was ten-thirty.

"How far are we from Yale?" she asked.

"The university? About twenty-five miles," the woman said. "My son goes there. It takes him about twenty minutes or so."

Blair frowned. It had never occurred to her that the sons of the types of people who managed Motel 6es could go to *Yale*.

"How long is this jump-start thing going to take?"

Aaron handed the woman the clamps for the jumper cables. He laughed. "Oh, it could take anywhere from five minutes to two hours," he said, winking at the motel manager.

Blair crossed her arms over her chest. "We don't have two hours!"

Aaron opened the door to the Saab and started the engine, revving the gas a few times to make sure it was well and truly fired up to go. He left the engine running and motioned for Blair to get in.

"You're lucky," he said, and winked at the hotel manager again. She switched her car off and Aaron removed the cables, closed the Saab's hood, and got in next to Blair. He pulled an envelope out of his jacket and handed it to her.

Blair ripped it open. It was a cheesy Hallmark card with a picture of a little girl on it. TO MY SISTER, it read. ON HER SPECIAL DAY.

"Ready?" Aaron said.

Blair closed the card. "Just drive, please," she ordered. She touched the zit on her forehead. It felt like it was growing exponentially with each minute that passed.

What's your biggest strength?

I never give up.

And your biggest weakness?

I'm a little impatient. But only a little.

Yeah, right.

j makes nice

"Why don't you go out for a run or something?" Rufus Humphrey suggested to his daughter on Saturday morning. He scratched at the gray wiry hair sticking out in tufts at the neckline of his yellowed undershirt. "Your mother was a runner."

Jenny scowled. She hated talking about her mother. "Mom only ran with her personal trainer. They were sleeping together, remember?"

Her father shrugged. "You look bored, that's all," he said. "Want to go to the movies with me?"

"No," Jenny said. She sipped her tea. "I'd rather just stay here and watch TV."

"Fine," her father said. "Just make sure it's something educational. You know, like *Sesame Street*." He smacked the top of Jenny's head with the Saturday *Times* and headed into the bathroom.

Jenny stayed seated at the kitchen table, staring into her mug. Marx, their overweight tabby cat, leapt up onto the table and sniffed her ear.

"I'm bored," Jenny told him. "Are you bored?"

Marx sat down and licked his enormous belly. Then he jumped off the table and headed for his bowl of cat food.

When in doubt, eat.

Jenny stood up and opened the refrigerator door. She stood there for a while, staring into it. Swiss cheese. A grapefruit. Sour milk. A box of cornflakes put in the fridge to hide it from the roaches. A lone English muffin.

The phone rang.

Jenny didn't move. No way was it for her, anyway. Nate, Dan, Serena—they were all away.

It rang again and again and again.

"Jenny, dammit!" she heard her father yell from the bathroom.

Jenny slammed the fridge closed and picked up the phone.

"Hello?" she said.

"Hey, Jennifer, it's Vanessa."

"Hey," said Jenny.

"Is Dan around?"

"No. Dan went up to Brown with Serena for the weekend. He didn't tell you?" Jenny said.

"No."

"That's weird," Jenny said.

"Yeah. We haven't really been speaking that much lately," Vanessa said.

"Oh." Jenny walked back to the fridge and opened it again. Swiss cheese. She could have Swiss cheese melted on the English muffin.

"Okay, well, I guess if he's not there, he's not there," Vanessa said. She sounded really disappointed. Disappointed and hurt.

Vanessa's whole charade with her cool, older boyfriend didn't fool Jenny for a minute. Vanessa was totally in love with Dan. If Dan told Vanessa he'd marry her if she grew her hair out, wore bright colors, and got some exercise, Vanessa would do it. Jenny felt kind of sorry for her.

Jenny put the Swiss cheese back on its shelf. "Hey, I have kind of a weird question," she said, deciding to be nice. "Do you want to like, do something today? I mean, together?"

There was a brief little pause. The sound of Vanessa hesitating.

"Sure," she said. "I'm holding a screening of my film at The Five and Dime at noon. You could come to that and we could hang out afterwards or something."

Jenny closed the refrigerator and leaned against it. Vanessa wasn't exactly her favorite person in the world, but what else was she going to do with Nate gone? "All right," she said. "I'll see you there."

Who knew? She and Vanessa might even wind up becoming friends.

the interview: how to make an impression

"Thank you for waiting," Blair's interviewer said, sweeping into the cold blue waiting room of the Yale admissions office, where Blair had been sitting stiffly on the edge of a wing-back chair for over fifteen minutes. Aaron had almost hit several people getting her there on time, and then she'd had to wait. Now she was a nervous wreck.

"Hi!" Blair squeaked, jumping to her feet. She thrust out her hand. "I'm Blair Waldorf."

The interviewer, a tall, tanned man with gray hair at his temples and sparkling green eyes, took her hand and shook it. "So glad to meet you. I'm Jason." He turned and led Blair into his office. His pants were a little tight in the ass, Blair noticed. "Have a seat," he said, crossing his legs and pointing to the blue velvet armchair across from him.

He reminded her of her father.

Blair sat down and crossed her legs. She had to pee. There were cat hairs on her skirt that she hadn't noticed before.

"So, tell me about yourself," Jason said, smiling at her with his nice green eyes. Green, like Nate's.

"Um," Blair said. She couldn't remember if this was one of the questions she'd prepared for or not. It seemed so vague. *Tell me about yourself.* Tell him what?

She twirled her ruby ring around and around on her finger. She really, really had to pee.

Blair took a deep breath and began talking. "I'm from New York City. I have a younger brother. My parents are divorced. I live with my mom, who's getting remarried soon, and my dad lives in France. He's gay. He loves to shop. I have a cat, and my new stepbrother Aaron has a dog. My cat hates the dog, so I don't know how it's going to work out." She stopped for breath and looked up. She realized that the entire time she'd been speaking she'd been staring at Jason's black lace-up shoes. This was a no-no. She was supposed to make eye contact. She was supposed to make an impression.

"I see," Jason said pleasantly. He jotted a few things down on his pad.

"What are you writing?" Blair asked, leaning forward to look.

Good grief, surely that was another no-no.

"Just a few notes," Jason said, hiding what he'd written with his hand. "So tell me why you're interested in Yale."

This one she'd prepared for.

"I want the best. I am the best. And I deserve the best," Blair said confidently. She frowned. That didn't sound right. What was wrong with her? "My dad went to Yale, you know," she added hastily. "He wasn't gay then."

Jason frowned and scribbled away. "Yes, he did, didn't he?"

Blair yawned discreetly into her fist. She was extremely tired, and her shoes hurt like hell. She uncrossed her legs, rested her elbows on her knees, and slipped her heels out of her shoes. That was better.

Except that now she looked like she was sitting on the toilet.

As he wrote, Jason's gold monogrammed cufflinks gleamed in the cold November light coming through the window.

Blair's father had worn cufflinks like that the night he took her out for her birthday. The night all hell broke loose.

"Can you tell me about a favorite book you've read recently?" Jason asked, looking up.

Blair stared at him, scanning her brain for the title of a book—any book—but she couldn't think of a single one.

Winnie the Pooh? The Bible? The *dictionary* for God's sake—it's really not that hard.

Then something clicked in Blair's brain. Or rather, her brain switched off completely and something else took over.

This is not recommended during an important college interview.

"I haven't been able to read much in the last few months," Blair confessed, her lip trembling. She closed her eyes, as if in pain. "Everything is a mess."

She was back—the leading lady in the tragic film that was her life. She imagined herself staring out to sea on a deserted beach wearing a trendy, short black trench coat. Rain and salt water pelted her face, mingling with her tears.

"I stole a pair of pajamas," Blair continued dramatically. "For my boyfriend. I don't know what made me do it, but I think it's a sign, don't you?" She glanced at Jason. "Nate didn't even thank me."

Jason shifted uncomfortably in his chair. "Nate?"

Blair snatched a Kleenex from the box on his desk and blew her nose noisily. "I've thought about ending it all," she declared. "I'm serious, I have. But I'm trying to be brave and hold on."

Jason had stopped writing. A boy sprinted by the window, wearing a Yale sweatshirt. "And what about sports? Are you interested in sports?"

Blair shrugged. "I play tennis. But the only thing I'm

really interested in right now is starting over. Beginning a new life," she said. She slipped her right shoe off entirely, placed her right foot on her left knee, and began massaging her toes. "It's been so hard," she added tiredly.

Jason put the cap on his pen and tucked it into his shirt pocket. "Er . . . do you have any questions for me?"

Blair stopped rubbing her toes and put her foot back on the floor. She scooted her chair forward and reached out to touch Jason's knee. "If you can promise me to let me in early, I promise to be the best student Yale University has ever had," she said earnestly. "Can you promise me that, Jason?"

Oh. My. God. Goodbye Yale University, hello community college!

Jason groped in his pocket, retrieved his pen, and scribbled something else on his pad, underlining it twice.

Let's guess what he wrote. *FREAKSHOW?*

"I'll see what I can do," Jason said. He stood up and held out his hand once more. "Thanks so much for coming in." He shook Blair's hand. "Good luck."

Blair wriggled her feet back into her shoes and smiled winningly at him. "See you next fall," she said.

And then she stood on tiptoe and kissed him on the cheek.

As if she hadn't already made enough of an impression.

guess who's getting into brown?

"I thought I'd feel more nervous," Serena said, stamping her feet in a pile of dried autumn leaves outside Corliss-Brackett House, the small brick building where the Brown University admissions office was located.

She had woken up in the hotel bed holding Nate's hand. When he'd opened his eyes a moment later, they'd smiled at each other, and Serena had known everything was going to be all right between them. There was still Blair to contend with, and they would never be as close as they once were. Things were different. But the look of distrust was gone from Nate's eyes, and so was the look of longing. She was just an old friend. She was safe.

"I'm not nervous, either," Nate said. "I mean, what's the worst that can happen—they don't take me? So what?"

"Yeah," Dan agreed, although he really was nervous. He felt clammy and shaky and completely overcaffeinated. He'd sat in the lobby of the Best Western for two hours that morning, reading the paper and drinking cup after cup of coffee, while the others took their time waking up. He took one last drag on his Camel before chucking it into the bushes. "Ready to go inside?"

"I feel like we should say some kind of cheer or something before we go in," Serena said, pulling her coat around her.

"Or not," Nate said, punching her lightly on the arm.

"Ow," Serena giggled. She punched him back. "Meathead."

Dan scowled at his shoes. He hated how comfortable they were together.

Serena turned and kissed Dan on the cheek. "Good luck," she murmured.

As if he weren't nervous enough already.

Then she turned and kissed Nate, too.

"Break a leg," Nate said, opening the door.

Serena's interviewer was an older man with piercing blue eyes and a bushy gray beard. He didn't even bother to introduce himself. He just sat her down and began firing away.

"Got yourself kicked out of boarding school," he said, drumming his fingers on his sturdy oak desk as he peered at her file. He looked up and removed his glasses. "So what happened?"

Serena smiled politely. Did he have to start with such a touchy subject? "I just didn't get back in time for the beginning of senior year." She uncrossed her perfect legs and recrossed them again, hoping she hadn't flashed too much thigh. Her skirt was a little short.

The interviewer frowned, furrowing his stern gray eyebrows.

"I kind of extended my summer vacation," Serena explained. "They didn't like that." She put her thumb in her mouth to bite her nail and then quickly removed it. She could do this.

"I see. Where were you? Stuck on an island in the Pacific? Working for the Peace Corps?" the interviewer barked. "Building latrines in El Salvador? What?"

Serena shook her head, feeling suddenly ashamed. "I was in the South of France," she squeaked.

"Aha. French. Any good at it?" the interviewer asked. He put on his glasses again and glanced down at Serena's file. "All you New York private school girls start French in preschool, don't you?"

"Third grade," Serena said, tucking her hair behind her ears. She wasn't going to let this dude intimidate her.

"So your old school took you back after Hanover sent you packing?" he pointed out. "That was good of them."

"Yes," Serena said. Her voice sounded a little meeker than she would have liked.

The interviewer looked up. "And are you behaving yourself?"

Serena smiled her most winning smile. "I'm trying to."

Nate's interviewer's name was Brigid. She'd graduated last year and loved Brown so much she'd gotten a job in admissions. For extra cash she made cold calls in the evenings asking for donations to the alumni fund. She was supremely perky.

"So tell me about some of your interests," Brigid said with a bright, dimpled smile. She had close-cropped blond hair and was built like a gymnast. She perched on the edge of her desk, facing him, a little white notepad in hand.

Nate wriggled his butt around on the uncomfortable wooden chair opposite her. He hadn't put much thought into the interview process because he wasn't even sure if he wanted to go to college next year or not. He was just going to have to wing this.

"I guess my biggest interest is sailing," he began. "My dad and I build boats up in Maine. And in the summers I race. I'd like to crew for an America's Cup team. That's my goal."

Nate wondered if he sounded like some kind of lame sailboat geek, but Brigid nodded enthusiastically. "I'm impressed."

He shrugged. "I guess I probably put more work into sailing than school," he admitted.

"Well, when you're really passionate about something, you don't notice the effort. Hard work feels like fun," Brigid said. She smiled brightly and wrote something down in her pad. It was almost as if Nate had just validated one of her favorite tenets of perkiness.

Nate rubbed his knees and leaned forward. "All I'm saying is my grades probably aren't good enough for Brown," he said.

Brigid threw her head back and laughed, nearly unseating herself. Nate put out a hand to steady her.

"Thanks," she said, righting herself. "Listen, I totally flunked AP bio in high school, and I got in. I know it may come as a surprise, but Brown is about way more than grades. We're into interesting people, not robots with straight A's."

Nate nodded. Brigid was better at her job than she'd first let on. He felt like he'd practically told her that he wasn't interested in going to Brown, but she wasn't letting him get away with it. She was making him want to try.

"So, is there a sailing team here?" he asked.

Brigid nodded energetically. "The sailing team *rocks!*"

"So, you're a reader," Marion, Dan's emaciated interviewer remarked. She was perched on the edge of her chair, her stick legs wrapped pretzel-like around each other, as she scribbled notes on an index card. "Quick, name two books and tell me why you liked one better than the other."

Dan cleared his throat and swallowed. His tongue felt so dry and brittle he thought it might break off and fall to the floor. He wondered how Serena was doing in her interview. He hoped she was all right.

"*The Sorrows of Young Werther,* by Goethe," he said finally. "And Shakespeare's *Hamlet.*"

"Good," Marion said, writing something down. "Go on."

"I know he's supposed to be this brave soldier prince, but I think Hamlet's pathetic," Dan said. Marion's eyebrows went up. "Werther I could relate to more," Dan went on. "He's a poet. He lives in his head, but it's like he's . . . it's like he's in love with the world. He can't stop himself from writing about it."

"Do you really believe that Goethe's Werther is less pathetic than Shakespeare's Hamlet?" Marion asked.

"Yes," Dan said, feeling more confident now. "I know Hamlet has a lot on his mind. His dad was murdered, the girl he loves is losing her mind, his friends betray him, his own mother and his stepfather want him dead."

Marion nodded, clicking her pen open and shut. "That's right. And Werther's only problem is that he's in love with Lotte, who doesn't really love him back and who's already spoken for. He's completely obsessed with her. He needs to get a life."

Dan sucked in his breath. Marion seemed to have hit the nail on the head. It was impossible not to see it now. *He* was Werther, and Serena was Lotte. She wasn't in love with him. She was already spoken for—after all, he'd seen her holding hands with Nate.

And Dan . . . he needed to get a life.

Dan put his head in his hands, his whole body trembling. He was afraid he was about to cry.

"I have to say, I'm impressed with the confidence with which you discuss literature," Marion observed, scribbling more notes.

Dan didn't look up. Serena didn't love him. It was all so clear now.

Marion clicked her pen open and shut a few more times. "Daniel?"

★   ★   ★

Serena's interviewer pulled on his beard and narrowed his eyes at her. "Read any good books lately?" he asked.

Serena sat up straight, thinking hard. She wanted to impress him, but she had to name a book she was at least vaguely familiar with. "*No Exit* by Jean Paul Sartre?" she said hesitantly, remembering the book Dan had recommended that she hadn't even finished.

"That's not a book, it's a play," the interviewer said. "Full of complainers in hell."

"I thought it was funny," Serena insisted, remembering that Dan had said it made him laugh. "'Hell is other people,' and all that," she quipped. It was all she remembered from the book.

"Yes, quite. Well, maybe you're smarter than me," the interviewer said, although it was clear he didn't believe it. "Did you read it in French?"

"Mais bien sûr," said Serena, lying her ass off.

The interview frowned and wrote something down.

Serena pulled her skirt down over her knees. She had the feeling this wasn't going well, but she wasn't sure why. It felt like the interviewer hadn't really given her a chance, like he'd had something against her before she even walked into the room. Maybe his wife had just left him and she was French or had blond hair like Serena. Or maybe his dog had just died.

"What else do you do?" the interviewer asked vaguely. It didn't even sound like he was interested.

Serena cocked her head. "I made a film," she said. "It's kind of experimental. I'd never made one before."

"Trying new things, I like that," the interviewer said. He seemed to warm to her for a second. "So tell me what it's about. Describe it to me."

Serena sat on her hands to keep from biting her nails. How could she describe her film so that he'd get it? Even she didn't exactly get it, and she was the one who'd made it. She took a deep breath. "Well, the camera kind of follows me around, staying really close up. First it follows me downtown in a cab. And then I go to this great shop on Fourteenth Street and kind of walk around describing things. And then I try on a dress."

The interviewer frowned again, and Serena knew she'd sounded like a total airhead. She looked down at her black flats, kicking her heels together like Dorothy trying to wish herself back to Kansas from Oz.

"It's pretty artsy," she added feebly. "You kind of have to see it to know what I mean."

"I guess so," the interviewer said, barely masking his disdain. "So, do you have any questions for me?"

Serena scrambled for something to say that would turn the interview around. *Show them you're interested,* Ms. Glos always said.

She stared at the floor, tiny beads of nervous sweat forming on her eyelids. What would her brother do in this situation? He was always so good at getting out of jams. *Fuck 'em* was his favorite phrase.

Exactly, Serena realized.

She had done her best. If this guy wasn't interested in her for whatever reason, then fuck him. She didn't need Brown anyway. Sure Erik went there, but she could do her own thing and her family would just have to deal. Like Nate had said before they went in for their interviews, so what if she didn't get in? She could go someplace else.

She looked up. "What's the food like in the dining halls?" she asked, knowing perfectly well what a lame question it was.

"Probably not on par with what you were eating in the South of France," the interviewer replied with a sneer. "Anything else?"

"No," Serena said, standing up to shake his hand. As far

as she was concerned, the interview was over. "Thank you." She flashed him her best smile one more time and then walked out of the room, her chin held high.

She hadn't had her usual luck this time, but she was still amazingly masterful at restoring her cool.

"Okay, so tell me about something you read lately," Brigid said. "Like a book or an article. Something that interested you."

Nate thought about this. He wasn't a very big reader. In fact he barely skimmed the books he had to read for English. He certainly didn't read for pleasure. But she'd mentioned an article. . . . Surely there must be something.

Then he thought of it. He and his friends had passed around an article from the *Times* about a pot pill. It was pure THC. No chemicals, no stems, no rolling papers. Of course the pill was for sick people, but Nate and his friends had other things in mind.

"I read in the *Times* that they're making this pot pill that's pure THC," Nate began. "It's supposed to be for cancer and AIDS patients, to like, manage their pain. But it's really controversial. I guess everyone's worried about it making it to the streets. It's pretty interesting."

"It sounds fascinating," Brigid said. "What's THC stand for, anyway?"

"Tetrahydrocannabinol," Nate said without skipping a beat.

Brigid leaned forward eagerly, threatening to fall off the desk again. "The pill you're talking about—it's man-made; it originated in a lab, was created by intelligent scientists and is administered to sick people by highly trained doctors. And yet it may become the catalyst for a whole new world of drug dealing and crime."

Nate nodded. "Totally."

"You know, there's a concentration here at Brown called science and technology studies that follows that sort of development," said Brigid. "You should look into it."

"Okay," Nate responded. Again, he had the feeling that Brigid wasn't going to let him get away with not trying to get into Brown. She was just way, way into it.

"So, do you have any questions for me?" asked Brigid.

What the hell, Nate decided. He might as well go for it. "So even if my grades aren't that good, do you think I could still apply early?"

Blair would kill him for not even bothering with Yale, but Nate realized he didn't care what Blair thought anymore. It would really ease his mind if he could apply to just one school and get in and then decide whether or not to go. If he did go to Brown he could sail the boat he'd built with his dad down from Maine and keep it somewhere near school. How cool would that be? He took a deep breath and flexed his calf muscles. Wow, did he feel good.

"Definitely apply early," Brigid enthused. "It will really demonstrate your commitment. We love that."

"Cool," said Nate. "I'll do that." He couldn't wait to tell Jennifer how awesome Brown was.

"So, you write, too, don't you, Daniel?" Marion said gently.

Dan pulled his hands away from his eyes and glanced dazedly around the office. Marion had a lot of books about men and women and relationships on her bookshelf. He could imagine her all curled up in an armchair in her office, sipping bouillon and reading *Men Are from Mars, Women Are from Venus.*

Maybe he should ask her to borrow it.

"What sorts of things do you write?" Marion coaxed.

Dan shrugged dejectedly. "Poetry, mostly."

She nodded. "What sort of poetry?"

Dan looked down at his scuffed suede shoes. Heat crept up his neck and into his cheeks. "Love poems," he said. Oh God. He couldn't believe he'd sent that poem to Serena. She probably thought he was a stalking loser freak.

"I see," said Marion. She clicked her pen a few times, waiting for Dan to say more.

But Dan remained silent as he gazed out the window at the fiery fall foliage decorating Brown's distinctive-looking campus. He'd imagined himself and Serena strolling hand in hand along the college green, discussing books and plays and poetry. He'd imagined them doing their laundry together in the basement of their dorm, making out on top of the washing machine as their clothes spun round and round.

Now he couldn't remember why he'd wanted to go to Brown in the first place. It all seemed so pointless.

"Excuse me," he said, standing up. "I have to go."

Marion unwound her legs. "Are you all right?" she said, looking concerned.

Dan rubbed his eyes and headed for the door. "I just need some fresh air," he said. Opening the door, he held up his hand. "Thanks."

Outside, he smoked a cigarette and gazed at the Van Wickle Gates, the official entrance to the Brown campus. He'd read in the catalog that they were only used twice a year. They swung inward when a new group of freshmen began the year with convocation, and they swung outward to let the graduating class out after commencement.

Dan had imagined himself and Serena marching through the gates, arm in arm in their graduation robes.

He'd imagined so many things he wouldn't be surprised if Serena herself was a figment of his imagination.

Nope.

"Hey, Dan, let's get the fuck out of here," Serena called from the car. "My brother's getting a keg."

Dan stubbed out his cigarette. *Awesome, dude,* he thought sarcastically. He couldn't wait to drink beer and hang out with a bunch of guys at a college he wasn't going to get into because he'd just had a nervous breakdown in his interview. He was tempted to tell Serena and the others that he'd just grab a bus home.

But then he turned around and saw how the sun melted on Serena's golden head, how her pale fingers glistened on the steering wheel, how she smiled at him. It didn't make him forget all his troubles, but it was enough to make him walk up to the car and get in.

At least he'd have some new material for his depressing poetry.

war and peace

Jenny was glad she'd come to Vanessa's screening at The Five and Dime, because there was only one other person in the audience besides Clark. That didn't seem to bother Vanessa, though.

"Grab a seat," she told Jenny when she walked in. "We're just about to start." She walked to the back of the room and dimmed the lights. The TV over the bar flickered blue.

"Hold on," Clark said from behind the bar. "I have to take a leak."

The place smelled of stale cigarette smoke and spilled beer. A girl wearing blue leather pants and a black wife-beater T-shirt was sitting alone at the bar. There was a tattoo of a monkey on her bicep. Jenny sat down next to her.

"Hey," the girl said, holding out her hand, which was covered with silver rings. "I'm Vanessa's big sister, Ruby."

"I'm Jennifer," Jenny said. "I like your tattoo."

"Thanks," Ruby said. "Hey, I'm getting a Coke. You want one?"

Jenny nodded and Ruby swung her cool black bob around and shouted at the bathroom door. "Hey, bring us some Cokes, would you, man?"

Clark came out of the bathroom. "At your service!" he shouted back.

"I like to make him work for his money," Ruby joked.

Vanessa plunked herself down next to Jenny and kicked the legs of her bar stool impatiently. "Are we going to watch this or what?"

She'd shaved her head again recently. It was looking particularly domelike and odd. Jenny wondered if she should say something, like, "Nice haircut." But then she decided that would be weird.

Clark filled up two glasses of Coke and slid them across the bar. He hit play on the VCR and then came around to the other side of the bar and wrapped his arm around Vanessa's waist.

"And now for our feature presentation," he said, in a Mr. Moviefone voice.

Vanessa scowled. "Just watch," she said.

Jenny kept her eyes trained on the TV as the film began. The camera bopped along Twenty-third Street, following Marjorie Jaffe, a sophomore at Constance, as she walked toward Madison Square Park. Marjorie had frizzy red hair and was wearing a Kelly green scarf.

Kelly green is great if you wear it ironically. But Marjorie looked like she was actually serious about it.

Marjorie crossed the street and entered the park. Then she stopped, and the camera panned in on her face. She was chewing gum, slowly playing it between her teeth as her eyes scanned the park, looking for someone. At the corner of her mouth was an angry cold sore that she'd tried and failed to cover up with concealer. It looked pretty nasty.

Finally Marjorie seemed to find what she was looking for. The camera followed as she hurried over to a park bench. And on the bench was Dan.

He was lying on his back, one arm flung out, his fingers trailing the ground. His clothes were rumpled and his shoes were untied. A glass crack pipe lay on his chest, and there were bits of garbage stuck in his hair. The camera lingered on his still form. The sun was going down, and his cheeks glowed orangey pink in the light.

Jenny took a sip of her Coke. Actually, her brother made a pretty convincing junkie.

Marjorie knelt beside Dan and took his hand.

Dan didn't move. And then, slowly, his eyes fluttered open.

"Were you sleeping?" Marjorie said, peering at him. She smacked her gum a few times and wiped her nose on the back of her hand.

"No, I have been looking at you for a long time," Dan said quietly. "I knew by instinct that you were here. No one except you gives me such a sense of gentle restfulness . . . such light! I feel like weeping from very joy."

Jenny knew the movie was adapted from a scene in Tolstoy's *War and Peace*. It was kind of weird hearing her brother talk like someone out of the nineteenth century, but it was kind of cool, too.

Marjorie began tying Dan's shoes, still smacking her gum. She didn't look like she was trying to play a part. She was just sort of *there*. Jenny couldn't tell if that was intentional or not.

Before she could finish tying his shoes, Dan sat up and grabbed her wrists. The crack pipe rolled to the ground and smashed to pieces. "Natasha, I love you too dearly! More than all in the world!" he gasped, trying to sit up and then sinking back on the bench as if in pain.

"Easy there, soldjah," Marjorie said. "Don't have a coronary."

Ruby burst out laughing. "That girl is too much!" she cried.

Vanessa glared at her. "Shush," she said.

Jenny kept her eyes on the screen. Dan tried to reach for the crack pipe, but all that was left were shards of glass.

"Careful," Marjorie warned. She fumbled in her pocket and pulled out a stick of gum. "Here," she said, handing it to him. "It's wintagreen."

Dan took the piece of gum and laid it on his chest, as if he were too exhausted to unwrap it and put it in his mouth. Then he closed his eyes, and Marjorie took his hand again. The camera panned away, sweeping across the grounds of the park. It paused to watch a pigeon peck at a used condom on the ground, and then it hurtled west on Twenty-third Street, all the way down to the Hudson River, where it watched the sun set and disappear. Then the screen went black.

Vanessa got up and turned the lights back on.

"What was going on in the end with that pigeon and the condom?" Clark asked. He stepped behind the bar and pulled a bottle of Corona from the fridge. "Anyone want anything?"

"It's a mood piece," Vanessa said defensively. "It doesn't have to make perfect sense."

"I thought it was hilarious," Ruby said. She tipped her glass back and chewed on some ice. "More Coke, please," she told Clark.

"It wasn't supposed to be funny," Vanessa said angrily. "Prince Andrei is dying. Natasha will never see him again."

Jenny could tell Vanessa was trying very hard not to lose her shit. "I thought the cinematography was great," she said. "Especially those shots at the end."

Vanessa shot her a grateful look. "Thanks," she said. "Hey, you never saw the final cut of Serena's film, did you? It's pretty decent."

"Yeah," said Jenny. "But you did all the camera work for that, too, right?"

Vanessa shrugged. "Yeah. Pretty much."

"Seriously, though. Your film was good, but I liked *Planet of the Apes* better," Ruby joked.

Vanessa rolled her eyes. Her sister could be so immature. "That's because you're a moron," she snapped.

"I liked it," Clark said. He took a sip of his beer. "Although I didn't really get it."

"There's nothing to *get*," Vanessa said, exasperated.

Jenny didn't feel like sitting there listening to them argue. She'd come to Williamsburg to be entertained, not tortured. "Hey, do you want to go get some food somewhere or something?" she asked Vanessa.

Vanessa grabbed her coat off the bar stool and jammed her arms into it. "Definitely," she said. "Let's get out of here."

They walked to a café that specialized in Middle Eastern food and ordered hummus and hot chocolate.

"So, Jennifer. With a rack like that, how come you don't have like, seven boyfriends?" Vanessa said, pointing directly at Jenny's chest.

Jenny was too embarrassed to even realize how rude Vanessa's question was. "Well, I do . . . kind of . . . have one."

"Yeah?"

"Yeah. Sort of." Jenny blushed, remembering how Nate had been about to kiss her in the park. He'd promised to call her the minute he got back from Brown. Just thinking about it made her sweat.

The waitress brought their hot chocolates.

Vanessa scooted her chair forward and blew into her mug. "So tell me about this boy."

"His name is Nate, and he's a senior at St. Jude's," Jenny said. "He's kind of a stoner, but he's really sweet and totally unpretentious, you know, for a boy who lives in like, a billion-dollar town house."

Vanessa nodded. "Uh-huh." He sounded like the kind of boy she would never be remotely interested in. "And are you guys like, going out? Isn't he kind of . . . you know, *old*?"

Jenny just smiled. "Nate doesn't mind. He just . . . *likes* me." She blew happily into her mug, letting the steam hit her cheeks.

Vanessa was about to ask if Jenny was putting out for this Nate character. That might explain why he liked her so much.

"I mean, we haven't even kissed or anything yet," Jenny continued before she could ask. "Which kind of makes me like him even better. He's so *not slimy*, you know? He doesn't even stare at my chest."

"Wow," Vanessa said, impressed.

"Anyway," Jenny added, sipping her hot chocolate. "He's up at Brown this weekend. I wonder if he'll bump into Dan."

"Maybe." Vanessa shrugged, trying to act like she didn't care. She wished she didn't get all goose-pimply whenever anyone mentioned Dan's name.

The waitress brought their hummus, and Vanessa sank a piece of pita bread into it and swirled it around.

Jenny knew Vanessa still had a huge crush on Dan—her film was partly a testament to that. But Dan was with Serena now. And if Dan was with Serena, Jenny had access to Serena, which was just the way Jenny had always wanted it. Or was it?

Jenny dipped her pinky in the hummus, brought it to her mouth, and sucked on it, thinking. Dan was his usual miserable self whether he was with Serena or not, although Jenny had to admit she kind of missed him. And when she really thought about it, she realized she didn't need Serena to be going out with Dan to hang out with Serena. After all, she had helped Serena with her film. She could talk to her whenever she wanted. She wasn't Dan's little sister Jenny anymore. She was Jennifer, her own person, with a hot senior for a boyfriend.

She looked up and smiled at Vanessa. Maybe she could help her.

"You know, Serena tried to read one of Dan's favorite books," Jenny said. "And she totally hated it. She couldn't even finish it."

Vanessa frowned. "So?"

Jenny shrugged. "So I just don't think they have all that much in common, that's all."

Vanessa narrowed her eyes. "This coming from the girl who would practically lick the bottoms of Serena's feet if she asked you to."

Jenny opened her mouth to say something in her defense. Then she shut it again. It was true: she had been following Serena around like a little puppy dog. But not any longer. Her name was Jennifer now.

"I just think that if you still have feelings for Dan, you should do something about it, that's all. You might be surprised," Jenny said.

"I don't," Vanessa said quickly. She grabbed a triangle of pita bread and ripped it angrily in half.

"Yes, you do."

Vanessa didn't like being told what to do, especially by a little kid. But Jenny seemed sincere, and if Vanessa were to be honest with herself, she had to admit that she very definitely did still have feelings for Dan.

She ran her hand over her nearly bald head and raised her eyes to meet Jenny's. "You think?" she said.

Jenny cocked her head. Vanessa had pretty decent bone structure. With a little lip gloss she might actually look like a girl. She also wasn't half as tough or as weird as she made herself out to be.

"You might have to grow your hair out a little, but it could happen," Jenny said. "I mean, you guys are already really good friends. You just have to take it to the next level."

Give a girl a boyfriend and she becomes a total expert on relationships.

b freaks out in a major way

"So how'd it go?" Aaron asked when Blair came back to the car after her interview. He was sitting on the Saab's hood, softly playing his guitar and smoking another herbal cigarette. He looked right at home at Yale.

"Okay, I think," Blair said hesitantly. Reality had yet to set in. She opened the door to the passenger seat, sat down, and removed her shoes. "I think I have a blister. Fucking flats."

Aaron opened the driver's side door and got in. "So what'd they ask you?" he said.

"You know, why Yale—stuff like that," Blair said vaguely. The whole interview was a blur to her now. She was just glad it was over.

"Sounds pretty standard," Aaron said. "I'm sure you did fine."

"Yeah." Blair turned and reached behind her for her bag. *The Selected Short Stories of Edgar Allan Poe* was lying on the backseat.

Blair remembered one of her interviewer's questions. *Can you tell me about a favorite book you've read recently?*

Uh-oh.

Suddenly it all came back to her.

She whipped around, trembling. "Shit," she said, in almost a whisper.

"What?"

"I messed up. I completely fucked up the whole thing."

"What do you mean?" Aaron asked, confused.

Blair rubbed the pimple above her eyebrow. "He asked me if I'd read any good books lately. Do you know what I said?"

Aaron shook his head. "What?"

"I told him I hadn't been reading anything because my life is a total mess. I told him I shoplifted. I told him I was suicidal."

Aaron just stared at her, his eyes wide.

Blair gazed out the window at Yale's pretty campus. She'd wanted to go there since she first came with her father to watch the Yale versus Harvard football game on alumni weekend when she was six. Yale was her destiny. It was everything she'd worked for. Why she didn't go out on weeknights anymore because she was actually studying for her APs. She'd been so confident about getting in, and in a few short minutes she'd blown it completely. How could she face everyone after this?

Aaron put his hand on her shoulder. "So are you? Suicidal, I mean?"

Blair shook her head. "No." She slumped in her seat, her chest heaving as angry tears rolled down her cheeks. "Although I should be after this."

"And do you really shoplift?"

"Shut up," Blair snapped, shrugging his hand off her shoulder. "This is all your fault. You kept me up too late. I should have just taken the train up this morning like I'd planned to. "

"Hey, I didn't tell you to say all those things in your interview," Aaron corrected her. "I wouldn't worry about it so much, though. The interview only counts for like one fifth of the whole process. You might still get in. Even if you don't, there are a billion other good schools to go to."

Blair considered this. She tried to remember how the rest of the interview had gone. Maybe that one little blip hadn't mattered as much as she thought.

Then she remembered what she'd done at the end of the interview.

Blair slammed her head against the back of her seat. "Oh God!"

Aaron put the key in the ignition and started the engine. "What?"

"I kissed him."

"Who?"

"The guy. The interviewer. I kissed him on the cheek before I left," Blair said. Her lower lip trembled and more tears rolled down her face. "I was a total freakshow."

"Whoa," Aaron said, sounding slightly impressed. "You kissed your interviewer? I bet you're like the first person who's ever done that."

Blair didn't answer. She turned her body toward the window and wrapped her arms around herself, crying miserably. What would she tell her father? What would she tell Nate? She'd given him such a hard time about not being serious about Yale, and then she'd gone and turned her own interview into a complete farce.

"Okay, you know what?" Aaron said, backing the car out of the lot. "I think we should get the hell out of here before they call the cops or something." He smiled and picked up a dirty Dunkin' Donuts napkin from off the floor, handing it to Blair to blow her nose with. "Here."

Blair let the napkin drop to the floor. She couldn't imagine how she'd gotten herself into this situation in the first place. Riding around in a dirty car with an overly optimistic dreadlocked vegan boy who was soon to become her stepbrother. Staying up late eating junk food and drinking beer. Spilling her guts to her Yale interviewer and then kissing him and totally wrecking her future. These sorts of things didn't happen to her. They happened to losers with problems. The actors who showed up time after time at castings but never got the leads. People with bad hair and skin problems and horrible clothes and no social skills. Blair touched the zit on her forehead once more. Oh God. What was she turning into?

"Want to go get breakfast somewhere?" Aaron asked, turning onto the main road through New Haven.

Blair slumped down in her seat. She couldn't bear to eat anything ever again. "Just take me home," she said in disgust.

Aaron put on a Bob Marley CD and drove toward the highway, while Blair stared out the window, trying to think of reasons to live.

There was the Constance film festival on Monday. If she won she'd have one more accolade on her record, and maybe Yale would turn a blind eye to her unfortunate interview. Maybe they'd forgive her for being weird, because, after all, she was an artiste. And if she won the competition but *still* didn't get into Yale, she could become all artsy and start wearing only black like that weirdo Vanessa and apply to NYU or Pratt. And if she didn't win? She'd have one more thing to add to her list of reasons why her life was totally fucked up.

To makes things worse, next weekend was her mother's spa day and bridesmaids' luncheon. Blair was going to have to be pleasant and enthusiastic. She might even have to talk to Serena. *Yippee!*

And *then* the following Saturday was the wedding day

itself. Her birthday. And the day she was finally supposed to lose her virginity to Nate. Blair squeezed her eyes shut as tight as they would go, trying to recall the image she'd dreamed up earlier of Nate uncorking a bottle of champagne in their hotel suite, wearing those sexy cashmere pajama bottoms. Instead her head was filled with an entirely different vision. She imagined Aaron's dog trotting up to her with a letter in his slobbery mouth. The letter was written on Yale stationery and it read, "Dear Ms. Waldorf, We regret to inform you that you have been denied admission to Yale. Thanks for trying, and have a nice life. Sincerely, Yale University Office of Admissions."

Blair opened her eyes and sucked in her breath. *No*, she told herself firmly. She wasn't a loser. She was going to get into Yale, no matter what. She and Nate were going to go there together. They were going to live together and do it whenever they wanted to. That was the life she had imagined for herself and that was how it was going to be.

She turned to Aaron. "First thing when we get back, I'm calling my dad and asking him to donate something to Yale," she said determinedly. It wasn't exactly bribery, was it? That sort of stuff happened all the time! And it wasn't like she was a bad student or anything.

Still, her interviewer definitely wasn't going to forget that kiss anytime soon. Whatever her father donated was going to have to be pretty huge.

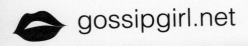

gossipgirl.net

topics ◄ *previous*   *next* ►   *post a question*   reply

Disclaimer: All the real names of places, people, and events have been altered or abbreviated to protect the innocent. Namely, me.

hey people!

WHO'S WITH WHO?

Has **D** completely given up on **S**? Is **S** blowing **D** off on purpose or just being oblivious in that fabulous way of hers? And is **N** actually serious about **J**? I mean, is he really going to ditch **B** in her time of need? For a ninth-grader?? Place your bets now.

YOU KNEW THIS WAS COMING

Yale University has just announced the addition of the Yale Waldorf Vineyard, and a new minor in wine management has been added to the curriculum. Students will produce their own wines, which will be sold by local merchants with the university's name on the label. Each semester a group of students will live and work at the university's new vineyard in Southern France, mastering the art of making wine, eating French food, and speaking French like natives. The vineyard will be up and running this summer, thanks to a generous donation by a prospective parent.

It looks like Daddy came through with the goods, but **B**'s still going to have to wait until April to see if she got in, just like the rest of us. The suspense is killing me!

Your E-Mail

Dear GG,
I've heard a few thing about all the films entered in the school film festival. (I go to Constance, too.) Anyway, I think **B** should win. I'm serious. I know her film sounds kind of repetitive, but it's supposed to be like this very cool MTV video effect. I'm in her film class and she's the best at editing, so I bet it's pretty

cool. *S* doesn't even know how to turn on a camera, and *V*'s films are always so pretentious. That's it.
—RainyDay

Dear RainyDay,
I thought *B*'s film sounded pretty out there, but I'm willing to take your word for it. It's up to the judges to decide on Monday. And the losers are bound to vent their disappointment in some outrageous fashion. I can't wait!
—GG

Sightings

J and *V* shopping at **Domsey's** in Williamsburg. *V* actually bought a vintage little black dress. She must be serious about showing *D* that she cares. *B* and *A* bumping into her mother, his father, and their wedding planner on the way into their building on Seventy-second Street. *B* did not look happy. *D, S, N,* and friends piling out of **Grand Central** on Sunday afternoon. All six looked pretty hungover, but what's new?

ONE LAST THING

It's Thanksgiving time, time to give thanks for what we have. So . . . thank you for all the nice leather pants at Intermix and the amazing leather car coat I got at Scoop. Thank you to every boy I know and those I haven't met yet for getting cuter and cuter with age. And thank you everyone for constantly misbehaving and always giving me something to talk about.

More soon.

You know you love me,

gossip girl

and the winner is . . .

Mrs. McLean, the Constance Billard School headmistress, had given the edict that the upper-school girls would be excused from their last two classes on Monday to attend the senior film festival. Grades seven through twelve filed into the auditorium and took their seats. A large white screen hung from the ceiling over the stage. The contestants sat in the front row, Blair, Vanessa, and Serena among them. Arthur Coates, Isabel's famous actor father, stood at the podium, ready to give a speech and introduce the films.

Serena sat at the end of the front row near the window, watching smartly dressed passersby parade across Ninety-third Street. Her nails were already chewed ragged, and she'd worried a tiny run in her black tights into a major run that traveled from her ankle up to her thigh.

Of course, she still looked good. She always did.

But Serena was nervous. This was her one extracurricular project. Winning the competition was the only way for her to show colleges that she was more than just a girl who got kicked out of boarding school because she couldn't be bothered to get back in time for the first few weeks of classes, or a girl whose grades were less than spectacular. She wasn't a total screwup. She was creative. She had substance. She had taste. And if they couldn't see that, then fuck 'em. . . . *Right?*

Vanessa was nervous, too, although she didn't let on. She sat slumped in her chair, digging *X*'s into the top of her black three-ring binder, glaring over the tops of her Doc Martens at the auditorium's wood floor. She didn't care if Ruby and Clark didn't get her film. Jenny said she liked it. And even if the story hadn't really worked out the way she'd wanted it to, and the chemistry between Marjorie and Dan had been less than sizzling, the cinematography was excellent. Even before she started making the film, she'd counted on winning the competition. It was going to clinch her early acceptance to NYU.

Blair felt sick to her stomach for a variety of reasons. She'd been calling, e-mailing, and IMing Nate ever since she'd gotten back into the city on Saturday afternoon, and he hadn't replied. Last night she'd almost stormed over to his house to see what the deal was, but then her mother had dragged her to a tasting at the St. Claire Hotel to decide on food for her wedding. As if Blair could give a fuck whether the quenelle was too fishy or the salad dressing was too oily. After they had settled on four courses, she'd had to listen to her mother and the party planner have an inane discussion about whether or not the flower arrangements should be high or low—long-stemmed or short-stemmed. High meant people would have trouble seeing over them. Low meant they wouldn't look as impressive. They settled on in-between, as if that weren't the most *obvious* call in the world.

When she got home, her father had left a message on her machine asking how his Bear's Yale interview had gone. Blair didn't call him back. The memory of her lousy interview clung to her like a bad-smelling shadow, and she refused to discuss it with anyone. Talking about it would be like admitting defeat, and Blair wasn't ready for that yet. Instead, she sent her father a perky e-mail telling him all about how her interviewer was fascinated with wine and had been trying to add a wine management minor to the curriculum for years. She left out any mention of the actual interview, telling him only that a donation would secure her 'already pretty sure' place at Yale. With a few lines, she had her father dying to donate his entire estate. She was a master of persuasion.

Today the film competition brought another chance for her luck to change.

It had to change. It just *had* to.

"Thank you for coming," said Mr. Coates, smiling his notoriously ravishing smile. He had starred in a TV show in his teens, had a platinum album in his twenties, and made all sorts of sexy music videos. Now he was a movie star and did Pepsi ads. "Today I'm pleased to present the next generation of new talent in the film industry."

He went on to give a little talk about the history of women in film. Marilyn Monroe. Audrey Hepburn. Elizabeth Taylor. Meryl Streep. Nicole Kidman. Julia Stiles.

Then he introduced the first film: Serena's. The lights were dimmed and the film began to roll.

Nervous butterflies flitted inside Serena's stomach as she watched her film for what seemed like the hundredth time. Even so, the film seemed to hold up. In fact, she began to feel kind of proud of it.

"Um. Can you say weird?" Becky Dormand whispered to her posse of juniors.

"Oh my God. How slutty does she look in that dress?"

Rain Hoffstetter whispered to Laura Salmon in the back row, where the seniors were sitting.

"And you could totally see her naked boob in the dressing-room mirror," Laura whispered back.

When the picture faded to black and the lights came up, the audience applauded. It wasn't crazy, wild, screaming applause, but it was solid. Somebody whistled and Serena craned her neck to locate the whistler. It was Mr. Beckham, the film teacher. She wasn't even one of his students.

"I heard she didn't even make the film herself," Kati Farkas whispered to Isabel Coates. "She paid this famous director to do it for her."

Isabel nodded. "I think it was Wes Anderson," she said.

Next, Mr. Coates introduced two more films. First, there was Carmen Fortier's conversation with her ninety-four-year-old grandmother, which was mostly about the merits of watching *Sesame Street*, and didn't seem to make much sense. Next was Nicki Button's tour of her country house in Rumson, New Jersey, which was boring as hell, especially when she recited the names of all the stuffed animals she had collected over the years. Fluffernutter. Larry. Bow Wow. Horsie. Ralph. Pigsy-fucking-Wigsy.

Like, *Who the hell cared?*

The Constance girls clapped politely, and then Mr. Coates introduced Vanessa's film.

The minute Marjorie's frizzy red-headed form appeared on the big screen, Vanessa began giggling nervously. She rarely laughed or even smiled in public, but Marjorie was just so ridiculous she couldn't help it. Her whole body was shaking, and she had to look away. Next to her, Blair Waldorf crossed her legs in that bitchy way of hers and shot Vanessa a nasty glance. Then the camera moved lovingly over Dan's crumpled form and Vanessa stopped laughing. God, he was beautiful.

The room was quiet for a moment after the film ended. Then Jenny began to clap from where she sat with the rest of the ninth-graders. Mr. Beckham whistled loudly, and the room erupted in applause.

"Way to go, Marjorie!" a few sophomores shouted.

"That condom thing was really gross," Kati whispered to Isabel in the back of the room.

"What the hell *was* that?" said Laura.

"That girl is seriously deranged," said Rain.

Finally it was Blair's turn.

Blair clutched her PalmPilot to her chest as Audrey Hepburn ate her croissants over and over. In the back of the room her friends danced in their seats to the music and clapped loudly when the film was over.

"That was cool," Isabel told Kati. "Wasn't it?"

"Totally," Kati agreed.

"That was okay," Becky Dormand whispered to her friends. "I mean she probably didn't have that much time to work on it now that she's so busy filling out applications to like, every college on the East Coast."

"I heard that even if she gets into Yale, she has to defer her admission for a year so she can get like, some intense therapy," another junior girl said.

"You mean because of the thing with her stepbrother? I heard they've been sleeping together ever since he moved in," Becky said.

"*Gross!*" the other girls exclaimed.

Finally Arthur Coates stood up with a white envelope in his hand. "You know, there are no really winners or losers," he began.

Blair swallowed nervously. *Yeah, yeah, yeah. Just open the frigging envelope.*

"And the winner is . . ."

Heavy pause.

"Serena van der Woodsen!"

Complete silence.

Then Vanessa stood up and wolf-whistled like her sister had taught her. She was disappointed, but Serena's film was good, and fuck it—she was proud to have been a part of it. When she saw Vanessa, Jenny stood up, too, clapping loudly. Then Mr. Beckham stood and shouted, "Bravo," and the rest of the school joined in.

Serena walked up to the podium in a daze of happiness and accepted the award—two tickets to Cannes and three nights at a five-star hotel during the film festival in the spring. She hesitated, pushing her shimmering blond hair behind her ears and leaning into the microphone.

"I'd like two other girls to come up here," she said. "Vanessa Abrams and Jennifer Humphrey. I couldn't have done it without them."

Vanessa stuck her tongue out at Jenny from across the auditorium and then went up to the podium to join Serena. After all, she had done all the camera work. She deserved some fucking credit for making this whole thing possible.

Serena shook Vanessa's hand and handed her a plane ticket. "Thanks," she whispered. "I want you to have this."

Jenny crawled excitedly over her classmates' knees and joined Serena and Vanessa at the podium. Serena kissed her on the cheek and pressed the other plane ticket into her hand. "You're awesome," Serena said. Jenny blushed: she'd never stood up in front of an audience before.

This isn't happening, Blair thought. She sat stiffly in her chair and closed her eyes to drown out the applause. She was sleeping. It was only three in the morning. Monday hadn't even started yet. There were hours to go until she would step proudly up to the podium wearing her lucky lilac-colored cardigan and accept the prize from Mr. Coates.

Sorry.

Blair opened her eyes. Serena was still beaming annoyingly at the audience.

And Blair was still starring in the most depressing movie ever made. The movie that was her life.

tortured romantic can't say no

"I won!" Serena cried.

Dan kicked at a broken Snapple bottle on West End Avenue and clutched his cell phone to his ear. "Won what?" he said, trying not to sound interested.

"The senior film festival," Serena burbled excitedly. "They liked it! I can't believe it. Vanessa even said I should think about applying to art schools. I could be a filmmaker!"

"Good," Dan said. He couldn't think of a more appropriate response. Every time he heard Serena's voice or even thought about her, he felt like he was being tortured.

"Anyway, I just wanted you to know, since you've seen the film and everything," Serena said.

No response.

"Dan?"

"Yeah?"

"Just making sure you were still there. Anyway," she rattled on, "I have to do all this wedding stuff this weekend, so I may not be able to get together. But you're still coming to the wedding with me, right?"

Dan shook his head. *Tell her no,* his mind ordered him.

"You promised," Serena reminded him.

"Sure," he said. His heart won out every time.

"Cool," said Serena. "Okay, I'll call you later. 'Bye."

She clicked off. Dan sat down on the bottom step of someone's stoop and shakily lit a cigarette. Was he overreacting? Could it be that he had it all wrong? Maybe Serena did care, at least a little bit.

It was something to hope for.

And something to torture himself over.

j just tastes better

"So Brown was good?" Jenny asked Nate. They were sitting beside the boat pond in Central Park, watching little boys sail their toy boats past lazy ducks and floating leaves. Nate was holding her hand and it felt so nice Jenny didn't care whether they talked or not.

"Uh-huh," Nate said. "I mean, I still have to do well this term and write my essay and all that shit. But I really hadn't been thinking about school next year at all, you know? And now I'm kind of psyched." He held Jenny's hand up in front of his face and examined her tiny fingers.

Jenny giggled. "What are you doing?"

"I don't know. It's good to see you, though." Nate smiled at her. "Jennifer," he said. "I was thinking about you all weekend, and now here you are."

"Me too," Jenny said, smiling shyly. Again, she wondered if Nate was going to kiss her.

"I felt kind of bad before when we were in the park," Nate continued. "You know, when my friends showed up?"

Jenny nodded. *Yes?*

"There was something I wanted to do," Nate said. "And I should have just gone ahead and done it."

Yes, yes!

Nate pulled her toward him. They both kept their eyes open, smiling as they kissed.

Jenny had kissed two boys during a kissing game at a party once, but kissing Nate was the best moment of her entire life. She felt like she was going to explode with happiness.

Nate was surprised at how well she kissed. It definitely felt better than when he kissed Blair. Jennifer just tasted better. Like a sugar donut or a vanilla shake.

He pulled back, still gazing at Jenny's flushed and happy face.

Jennifer didn't know about Blair, and Blair didn't know about Jennifer. He'd been ignoring Blair's calls and basically pretending she didn't exist, but how long could he keep that up? Sooner or later Nate was going to have to talk.

He just wasn't sure what he was going to say.

sour milk pedicures

After some light shopping in the Chanel store on the ground floor, Eleanor Waldorf and her bridesmaids rode the elevator up to the Frederic Fekkai Beauté de Provence spa on Fifty-seventh Street. Blair, her mother, Kati, Isabel, Serena, and Blair's aunt Zo Zo were all there for their milk-and-honey foot and hand treatments, their sea mud facials, and, of course, to chat about the wedding. Afterward, they were having lunch at Daniel, Eleanor Waldorf's favorite restaurant. Blair's aunt Fran was meeting them there, forgoing the pedicure because she hated people to touch her feet.

The spa was like a busy restaurant, except it smelled like Frederic Fekkai shampoo and hair gel instead of food. It was big and bright, and employees rushed to and fro, servicing women in the beige hospital-type gowns that they wore to protect their clothes. Every one of the women had the same platinum and strawberry-blond highlights in her hair. It was the trademark hair color of the Upper East Side.

"Ciao, mes cheries!" cried Pierre, the skinny Japanese boy who worked in reception. "I've got three of you in pedicures while the other three are having your facials. Follow me, follow me!"

Blair didn't quite know how it happened, but she soon found herself seated between Serena and her mother with her hands and feet soaking in bowls full of warm milk and honey, while Kati, Isabel, and her aunt were having their facials in another section of the spa.

"Doesn't this feel nice?" Blair's mother cooed, sinking back in her chair.

"My milk smells off," said Blair. She wished she'd told her mom she'd meet everyone at the restaurant, as Aunt Fran had done.

"I haven't had a pedicure since the summer," said Serena. "My feet are so nasty I wouldn't be surprised if they turned my milk sour."

I wouldn't be surprised either, Blair thought bitterly.

"How do you want your nails?" her mother's manicurist asked as she massaged her fingers.

"I like them rounded, but not pointy," her mother advised.

"I like mine square," Serena told hers.

"Me too," Blair said, although she hated to say she liked anything Serena did.

Blair's manicurist slapped her wrist playfully. "You're so tense. *Relax,*" she said. "Are you the bride?"

Blair looked at her blankly.

"No, that's me," her mother answered cheerfully. "It's my second time," she whispered, winking annoyingly at the manicurist.

Blair felt her muscles tense up even more. How in hell was she supposed to relax?

"I saw these wonderful cashmere pajama bottoms in Barneys' men's department," her mother continued to babble. "I was thinking of getting a pair for Cyrus as a wedding gift." She turned to Blair. "Do you think he would wear them?"

Serena glanced nervously at Blair, wondering if she should say something. Now was her chance to bust Blair and get her back for being such a bitch. She could say something like, "Hey, Blair, didn't I see you *buying* a pair of pajama bottoms just like that at Barneys last week?" But Blair's face was turning redder and redder, and Serena didn't have the heart to say anything. Or rather, she had too much heart. Blair was already screwed up enough to have taken the pajama bottoms in the first place—Serena didn't need to screw her up even more.

"I don't know, Mom," Blair said miserably. Her neck felt itchy. Maybe she was having an allergic reaction and would have to be rushed to the hospital.

The manicurists finished massaging their hands and sat down on low stools to rub their feet and calves with lavender-scented oil.

"You never told me how your Yale interview went," Blair's mother said, her eyes blissfully closed.

Blair kicked a puddle of milk onto the floor.

"Careful," her manicurist advised.

"Sorry," snapped Blair. "It went great, Mom, really great."

Beside her, Serena let out a sigh. "I just had one at Brown this weekend," she said. "It was terrible. I think the interviewer was having a bad day or something. He was such a jerk."

Brown? Serena was at Brown last weekend? Alarms, sirens, bells, and whistles were all sounding loudly in Blair's head.

"I'm sure you did better than you think, sweetie," Mrs. Waldorf assured Serena. "Those interviews are so awful. I don't know why they put so much pressure on you girls."

Blair splashed another puddle of milk onto the floor. She couldn't keep still. She wished the manicurist would just let go of her leg. "When was your interview?" she asked Serena.

"Saturday," Serena said. She wasn't sure if she should mention that Nate was there, too. She had a feeling she shouldn't.

"What time on Saturday?" Blair demanded.

"Twelve," Serena replied.

Uh-oh.

"Nate had an interview there," challenged Blair. "His was at twelve on Saturday, too."

Serena took a deep breath. "Yeah, I know," she said. "I saw him there."

Blair flexed her foot in anger. *What the fuck?* The manicurist slapped it. "Relax," she warned.

"Nate hasn't called me since he got back," Blair growled. Her eyes narrowed as she stared at Serena's profile.

Serena shrugged. "Nate and I don't really talk anymore," she said. She certainly wasn't going to mention the fact that she and Nate had slept in the same bed in a hotel room and had woken up holding hands. Or that they had both gotten drunk at Erik's keg party and puked in the bushes behind his house together. They hadn't spoken since they got back to the city—that much was true.

"Where has Nate been, anyway?" Blair's mother yawned. The foot massage was putting her to sleep. "I haven't seen him in ages."

"Me neither," Blair hissed, and she was certain Serena had something to do with it. "I wonder why."

Serena knew Blair was waiting for her to make some sort of confession. She closed her eyes. "Don't look at me," she said. But the minute she said it she wished she hadn't. It was almost like she was asking for it.

Blair stood up abruptly, spilling her hand bowls of milk on the floor and nearly upsetting her foot bath.

"Shit!" the manicurist squealed, sliding off her stool and landing on her butt in a puddle of milk.

"Blair, what on earth?" her mother cried.

"Excuse me," Blair said tightly. Hot tears of rage gathered in her eyes. "I just can't sit here any longer. I'm going home." She glanced down at her manicurist. "Sorry about the mess," she said. Then she stamped out of the room, slipping slightly on the wet tile floor.

"What was that all about?" Blair's mother asked Serena. She was worried about her daughter, but she wasn't about to go after Blair and give up being pampered.

Serena shook her head. She had nothing to do with whatever problems Blair and Nate were having, although she was definitely curious. And she was kind of worried about Blair, too, despite how incredibly mean Blair had been to her lately. Blair appeared to be having some kind of breakdown.

"She's probably just nervous about the wedding," Serena said, although she was pretty sure that the wedding accounted for only a tiny portion of Blair's problems. "You know how she gets."

Blair's mother nodded. Did she ever.

topics ◀ *previous* *next* ▶ *post a question* *reply*

Disclaimer: All the real names of places, people, and events have been altered or abbreviated to protect the innocent. Namely, me.

hey people!

NOBODY DOES IT BETTER

Due to her dramatic departure, **B** missed her Frederic Fekkai facial, which is a shame, because few spas do it better. She also missed **K** and **I** getting drunk on white wine at Daniel and reassuring her mother that **B** and **N** hadn't consummated their relationship yet. She missed her aunts quizzing **S** about her college plans. And she missed an incomparable upside-down chocolate soufflé. Let's hope she doesn't miss the wedding—everyone will still have fun without her, but she's going to provide all the drama.

Your e-mail

Hey GG,
I heard **S** totally slept with like, all the judges on the film festival panel, so it's not really a big surprise that she won, know what I mean?
—ceecee

Hey ceecee,
She slept with all of them? Even the girls?
—GG

yo gossipgrl,
whassup? i just wanted to tell you that i think you are hot, even though we've never met. i'm a guy, by the way. i also wanted to say that i was in the park after school on wednesday and saw **J** and **N.** she's kind of hard to miss. i mean the top half of her is. they looked pretty happy to see each other if you know what i mean.
—goodie

Hi goodie,

Um, thanks for the compliment, I guess. Definitely thank you for the scoop. Word has it *N* and *J* have been hooking up after school every day. Poor *B.*
—GG

Sightings

B stalking the streets between *S*'s and *N*'s houses, trying to catch them in the act. *J* and *N* at the public library on Ninety-sixth Street, studying. How cute! *N* is clearly determined to get into Brown and into *J*'s . . . heart. *S* standing at her window wearing the brown **Chloé** dress *B*'s mom bought for all the bridesmaids. I know she's supposed to have the best figure on Fifth Ave., but I hear she was looking a little hippy. Too much junk food up in Rhode Island, perhaps? *N* picking up his wedding tux at **Zeller.** And *B* at a hockey game at **Madison Square Garden** with her brother and her new stepbrother. I guess even hockey was better than hanging out with her bride-to-be Mom or her perky bridesmaid friends. Now that's hard to believe.

Less than a week till the big day. Have a great Thanksgiving, but don't pig out too much, or you won't fit into your wedding duds!

You know you love me,

hot ushers and sexy bridesmaids

"This dress makes me look like I have silicone implants in my thighs," Kati complained, poking at her legs as she examined herself in the mirror.

"It makes my skin look totally gray," Isabel whined. She squirted some Lubriderm into her hands and smoothed it over her arms. "I should have bought that bronze body powder at Sephora," she added, pouting.

Blair rolled off the bed in their St. Claire Hotel suite and snatched up the Chloé dress, letting it dangle from her fingers. It was long and brown and sleek, with tiny pearlescent beads sewn diagonally across the bodice, and two delicate beaded strands, like necklaces, to hold it up.

She yanked off her white hotel bathrobe and pulled the dress on over her head. The material clung to her figure, but it didn't feel tight—it felt great. Blair examined herself in the mirror. The dress didn't make her look hippy at all. She looked *hot*. Yesterday she'd been waxed, plucked, exfoliated, steamed, and moisturized from her hair follicles down to her toenails at the Aveda Salon and Spa on Spring Street. She had new golden beige highlights in her hair, and her mother's makeup artist had dusted her entire body with sparkling scented body powder. Blair fluffed up her hair, which had just been blown out by her mother's hairstylist. She didn't care if Isabel and Kati weren't happy with their dresses, Nate wasn't going to be able to keep his hands off her tonight. Plus, the dress went perfectly with the Manolos her father had given her for her birthday. Blair pulled the shoes out of her bag and strapped them on. She was glad she could still be faithful to her dad, even at her mom's stupid wedding.

"You know you want me," Blair said to her reflection, pretending she was talking to Nate. She looked amazing, and she was definitely ready to do it.

"All set," Serena said, coming out of the bathroom in a cloud of sweet-smelling perfume. The dress looked pretty great on her, too, but Blair tried not to look. She had done a marvelous job of ignoring Serena all through hair and makeup that afternoon. She didn't see any reason to stop ignoring her now.

Someone knocked on the door. "Hey, it's me," Aaron said. "You guys ready?"

Blair opened the door. Aaron and Tyler were standing out in the hall wearing their tuxedos. Aaron had gotten his dreadlocks cut short so that they stuck out from his head in all directions. He looked like a rock star attending the Grammys. For once, Tyler looked like the perfect little gentleman, with neatly parted hair and a perfectly tied bow tie. She had to admit they both looked adorable.

"Wow," Aaron said. "That dress rocks."

Tyler nodded in agreement. "You look really good, Blair," he said earnestly.

Blair frowned, reveling in the attention. "You don't think it makes me look fat?"

What a drama queen.

Aaron shook his head. "Give it up, Blair," he said. "You know you're hot."

Blair grimaced. "You really think so?"

"Yeah," Aaron said. "Mookie thinks so, too. He told me. I had to leave him at home, but he'd definitely want to hump your leg in that dress."

"Fuck off," Blair growled, although she was enjoying every minute of it.

She turned to Kati, Isabel, and Serena. "Come on," she said. "Let's get this fucker over with."

As the girls filed out of the room, Blair glanced back at the suite's sumptuous king-sized bed. Okay, so the next few hours were going to be hell. And sure, she didn't know where in God's name she was going to college next year. But today was her birthday, and tonight she was going to lose it to Nate in that bed.

"Do you, Cyrus Solomon Rose, take Eleanor Wheaton Waldorf to be your lawful wedded wife, to love and serve, in sickness and in health, until death do you part?" asked the Unitarian minister from the altar of the intimate all-faiths United Nations Chapel.

"I do."

"And do you, Eleanor Wheaton Waldorf, take Cyrus Solomon Rose to be your lawful wedded husband, to love and serve, in sickness and in health, until death do you part?"

"Oh, yes. I do."

Misty Bass shifted her hips on one of the chapel's uncomfortable wooden benches. "Tell me again why they had to get married so quickly?" she whispered to Titi Coates.

Mrs. Coates moved closer to her friend and gave her a knowing glance through the little blue veil that was attached to her fabulous peacock feather cap. "I heard she was running out of money," she whispered. "It was her only way out of debt."

Mrs. Archibald couldn't help getting involved. "I heard she fell in love with his summer place in the Hamptons," she said, leaning forward to whisper in Misty's and Titi's ears. "She wanted it for herself, but he wouldn't sell. So she figured out another way to get her hands on it."

"How long do you think it will last?" Misty asked dubiously.

Titi smiled viciously. "How long could *you* live with *that*?"

They examined Cyrus Rose, who was looking particularly rosy in his gray pinstriped morning suit and cream-colored shirt, tie, and waistcoat. He'd worn a gold pocket watch and spats on his shoes.

Spats? What did he think this was, a costume party?

Eleanor looked radiant despite her ridiculous dusky pink Little Bo Peep gown. Her blue eyes gleamed with happy tears, and ancestral diamonds glittered from her neck, wrists, and ears.

But most importantly, the bridesmaids and ushers . . .

Blair clutched her bouquet of winter lilies and kept her eyes fixed on Nate, drowning out the wedding service completely.

A few days ago, Nate had finally sent her an oblique e-mail saying he was sorry he hadn't seen her in a while, but he'd had to go up to Maine to spend Thanksgiving with his family. Blair had responded immediately, telling him how nervous and excited she was about tonight. Nate had never replied, so she'd had to satisfy herself with the thought that all would be resolved when they saw each other again.

As long as that bitch Serena didn't get in the way.

Blair waited for Nate's eyes to shift to Serena so she could catch him staring at her yearningly. But Nate kept right on watching the ceremony, his green eyes sparkling in the candlelit chapel.

For once, Blair decided to be optimistic.

Maybe, just maybe, she was wrong about them. Forget Serena—Nate was as excited about tonight as Blair was. Why else would he be looking that good? He absolutely radiated sexiness.

But then again, so did she.

Her Chloé dress fit her body like a condom, and she was wearing absolutely nothing underneath it except for a pair of stay-up, lace-top stockings.

Oh, and her birthday Manolos, of course.

Blair was ready. She was a bouquet-carrying sex machine. *So why wasn't Nate looking at her?*

Nate watched the ceremony, feigning interest to avoid eye contact with Blair. He had noticed that she was looking particularly groovy, but all it did was make him worry about how he was going to handle things later on. In his pocket was Jennifer's favorite calligraphy pen, which she'd given him to remind him of her while he was gone for Thanksgiving. Nate couldn't bring Jennifer to the wedding, for obvious reasons. But he'd promised to meet up with her at the hotel bar during the reception so she could see him in his tux. He'd also promised her that he'd refrain from smoking a big fat joint before the wedding. Now he regretted it. He was going to have to face Blair completely sober. Nate stuck his hand in his pocket and gripped the pen. It made him jittery just thinking about it.

Serena felt jittery, too, although you'd never know it. Whenever a professional got his hands on her face with makeup and blew out her hair, the results were unreal. Her golden hair shone, her skin gleamed, her cheeks glowed, and the brown Chloé dress hugged her body, accentuating her narrow hips, the curve of her back, and her long, graceful legs.

But inside, Serena was a little messier.

First and foremost, she was worried about Dan. He was acting strange.

She hadn't been able to see him at all before the ceremony, but she had talked to him last night. Sort of. She'd done all the talking. Dan had kind of grunted at her and said he'd see her at the wedding. Serena didn't know what was going on with him, but there was definitely something.

She was also worried about Blair, despite the fact that Blair had been ignoring her all day. The girls were standing next to each other, and Serena could practically feel the tension zinging off of Blair's body like static electricity.

Across the aisle, Serena's brother Erik winked at her. He looked like a prince in his tux. A male version of Serena, all golden haired, blue eyed, and tall, with a sprinkle of freckles on his nose and adorable dimples in his cheeks. Serena had told him all about her crappy Brown interview, and predictably Erik had said two words in response: "Fuck 'em."

It wasn't exactly the most reassuring piece of advice she'd ever gotten, but Serena respected her brother's carefree brand of wisdom—it worked for him. And she was seriously considering art school now anyway.

She turned her head and tried to locate Dan in the audience, but she couldn't see his brown tousled hair anywhere among the glamorous hats and crisply coiffed dos of the wedding guests. She wondered if he'd even bothered to come.

Dan was slumped in a pew in the back, his hands sweating like crazy, trying not to listen to the ruthless gossip going on around him.

"It's even tackier than I expected," he heard a woman whisper.

"What on earth is she wearing?" her neighbor whispered back.

"What about *him?*" the first woman replied.

"And the bridesmaids' dresses. They're pornographic!"

Dan didn't know what they were talking about. Everyone in the wedding party looked pretty spectacular to him, particularly Serena. Dan had tried to clean himself up as best he could, but his scuffed black loafers were all wrong and his shirt wasn't even ironed properly. He'd never felt more out of place in his life.

But she'd wanted him there and there he was. A lamb ready for slaughter.

"And now, you may kiss the bride," announced the minister.

Cyrus grabbed Eleanor around the waist. Blair clutched her bouquet against her stomach to keep from puking.

It wasn't a very long kiss, but any public display of affection between people your parents' age is enough to make you gag.

Cyrus stamped on a wineglass wrapped in a napkin and the piano player pounded out congratulatory chords.

At last, they were married!

The wedding party followed the couple down the aisle and through the chapel doors.

Out on the sidewalk on First Avenue, across from the UN, Blair tiptoed up behind Nate and breathed into his ear. "I missed you," she purred.

Nate spun around and did his best to smile. "Hey. Congratulations, Blair," he said, kissing her on the cheek.

Blair frowned. "What for? This is like, the worst day of my life." She stepped closer to him. "Unless you make it better."

Nate kept right on smiling. "What do you mean?"

Blair was too fed up with things to mince words. She got straight to the point. "I mean," she said, "I'm not wearing any underwear."

Nate stopped smiling. "Okay." He rammed his hands in his pockets, fingering Jenny's pen.

"You haven't even wished me happy birthday yet," Blair pouted, sticking out her lower lip. She reached out and patted Nate's pockets. "And you haven't given me a present, either."

Nate's hand closed around the pen, hiding it from her.

"Why don't you ask that guy if he'll take our picture?" he suggested desperately.

The *Vogue* photographer was busily snapping romantic shots of Cyrus and Eleanor in the back of their Bentley. Blair went over and tugged on his sleeve.

"Take a picture of me and my boyfriend?" she asked him peppily.

But when she turned around, Nate was gone.

Down the block, Serena was waiting for Dan to emerge from the chapel, just like she'd promised. He came out and shuffled up to her, his head bowed.

"Sorry about that," Serena said, giving him a little hug. "Hope it wasn't too weird."

Dan shoved his hands in his tuxedo pockets. "It was okay."

"Well *I* thought it was weird," Serena said. "And I know these people."

She seemed so genuinely grateful that he was there Dan decided to loosen up a bit. "You look really great," he said.

Serena smiled. "So do you. Come on," she said, pulling him over to a waiting limo. She pushed him into the back seat. "Let's go get drunk."

They had the car to themselves. Dan loved the way the leather seats smelled. He sat close to Serena. Their legs were touching.

"Thanks for coming with me," Serena said.

Dan turned his head and their eyes met. The car was about to pull away from the curb. Serena had the feeling Dan was about to say something serious.

Then the door to the backseat opened and Nate popped his head in.

"Hey, guys," he said breathlessly. "Mind if I ride with you?" No way was he getting stuck riding in a car alone with Blair.

Erik appeared behind him. "Me too?" he said. He tossed a bottle of peach schnapps onto the seat. "I brought beverages."

Serena scooted over to make room. "The more the merrier!" she said gleefully.

Dan didn't say anything.

He lit a cigarette.

reception ain't no party

"You must be thrilled."

"Congratulations, dear!"

Blair hadn't factored the receiving line into her script for this evening's movie, and her mother and Cyrus seemed hell-bent on prolonging the agony. Her face hurt from smiling, and she was sick of people kissing her and making her tell them how happy she was for her mom. *As if.* It was bad enough that she'd already been forced to pose for the camera with her lips pressed against one of Cyrus's fat, ruddy cheeks. *Nasty.*

"She's really cool to hang out with," Blair heard Aaron tell someone. He was standing next to her on the receiving line and he kept telling people how psyched he was to have such a cool new sister. Blair knew he was being sarcastic. She wanted to hit him.

Happy birthday to me, happy birthday to me, Blair thought bitterly. As soon as this receiving line bullshit was over, she was going to find Nate and have a serious talk with him. Didn't he understand how much she needed him right now? Couldn't he see?

"At least they got this right," Misty Bass whispered to her husband when they passed through the receiving line and entered the elegant ballroom of the St. Claire Hotel, where the wedding reception was to take place. The room sparkled with silver, white linen, crystal, and candlelight. A harp player sat in the corner, playing discreetly. Waiters in white jackets distributed flutes of golden champagne and escorted guests to their appointed tables.

If Blair had involved herself in the seating arrangements, things might have been slightly different, but Serena, Dan, Nate, and Erik were all seated at the same table, with Serena sitting between Nate and Dan. Across the table from them was Chuck Bass, Serena and Dan's least favorite person in the entire zip code. He had shellacked his dark hair back with gel, which was a new look for him. It made him look like more of a penis man than ever.

(Penis man, *noun:* An insensitive, arrogant, annoying jerk. Usually, but not always, short and bald. Thinks he's the studliest dude in the room.)

Chuck was actually devastatingly handsome, in an aftershave commercial kind of way. It was his personality that made him a penis man.

On either side of Chuck were Kati and Isabel, still squirming in their too-tight dresses.

Dan sat down at his place and eyed the array of silverware.

"It's not that hard," Chuck told him snottily. He pointed at Dan's soup spoon. "Just work your way from the outside in."

"Thanks," Dan said miserably. He wiped his clammy hands on his tuxedo pants. He should never have come.

The waiters brought the first course. Pumpkin bisque, in honor of Thanksgiving, and a big basket of warm sourdough rolls.

"So I'm confused here," Chuck continued, dominating the table in his usual obnoxious way. He pointed his bread knife at Serena. "Are you with him?" he asked, jabbing his knife at Nate. "Or him?" he thrust his knife at Dan.

Erik laughed. "Actually, Chuck," he said sarcastically, "they're a threesome. Nate's had the hots for Dan forever. Serena introduced them."

Serena stirred her soup up and rolled her eyes apologetically at Dan. "Dan's my date," she said. "And he's probably hating me right now."

Dan shrugged. "No, I'm not."

But he wondered what the real answer to Chuck's question was. *Are you with him?* Well, was she? *Was she?*

Finally all the guests had passed through the receiving line, and Blair and her new and improved family made their way to the head table. Blair sat down between Aaron and Tyler, practically back-to-back with Nate. Blair couldn't believe it. Serena and Nate were sitting next to each other at the next table, while she was stuck sitting with her family. Un-fucking-believable.

She leaned back in her chair to whisper in Nate's ear. "Can I talk to you? After the speeches?"

Nate nodded hesitantly. He looked at his watch. Jennifer would be there soon. It was possible he could avoid talking to Blair altogether.

Satisfied, Blair tilted forward in her chair and scooped up her champagne flute, downing its contents in one giant gulp. If she was finally going to lose her virginity to Nate, she wanted to be relaxed.

"Easy there, princess," Aaron warned. "I don't want you puking all over me."

"Why not?" Blair replied, holding up her glass for the waiter to fill. "It would be an improvement."

Cyrus was reading from a stack of index cards and mumbling to himself, practicing his speech.

"Don't be nervous, darling," Eleanor said, patting his shoulder. "Just be yourself."

Blair rolled her eyes and downed another glass of champagne. That was the worst advice she'd ever heard.

The waiters cleared the soup bowls and poured more champagne. Cyrus Rose was sweating like a pig. He picked up a fork and banged it on his glass. Blair couldn't stand to sit there one agonizing minute longer. She sloshed champagne around in her mouth to clean it of any impurities, turned around, and tugged on the sleeve of Nate's jacket.

"Let's just go now," she said, between clenched teeth.

Nate turned around and stared at her.

"People, if I could just have a moment of your attention!" Cyrus said, still banging on his glass.

"Let's *go*, Nate," Blair ordered.

Nate looked at his watch. Jennifer was coming in a few minutes. No way was he going to keep her waiting because he was off somewhere letting Blair cry on his shoulder. "But Cyrus is making a speech," he said.

Blair dug her nails into his arm. "Exactly," she said. "Come *on*."

Nate shook his head. He took a deep breath and let it out. "Just relax," he told Blair and turned around.

Blair stared at the back of Nate's head in disbelief. "What?" she said, not sure if she'd heard him right. Her bare butt itched from her dress chafing against it. *This isn't happening,* she told herself. Nate wasn't acting like an asshole, and he didn't just majorly diss her. It was all in her head.

Cyrus cleared his throat.

"Blair!" her mother hissed from across the table.

Aaron grabbed her hand and pulled her around in her chair. "Don't be rude," he said.

The entire room was quiet, waiting for Cyrus to begin his speech.

"Thank you for coming," he began. "And thank you for cutting your Thanksgiving plans short so you could be here." Then he launched into the same lame-ass speech Blair had heard him practicing at home all week, pacing up and down the hallway of their Seventy-second Street penthouse in the same kind of cashmere pajama bottoms that she had stolen for Nate.

Blair sat very still, watching the bubbles float from the bottom of her champagne glass to the top. If she moved one muscle, her head was going to explode.

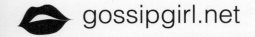

hey people!

NY TIMES WEDDING ANNOUNCEMENT

Eleanor Wheaton Waldorf, Upper East Side society hostess, and Cyrus Solomon Rose, real estate developer, were married today amidst scandal, gossip, and intrigue. They met in Saks last spring, and have been dating ever since. She was suffering from a major lack of confidence when they met, having recently been left by her first husband for another man. But Cyrus made her forget all that. He fell in love with her smile, her newly slimmed-down physique, and her huge Fifth Avenue apartment, and he wasn't going to let them go. He also couldn't wait to leave his plastic-surgery-crazed wife. Eleanor fell in love with Cyrus's cheery outlook on life, his naughty Santa Claus sex appeal, and his incredible Bridgehampton beach house.

How perfect for each other could they *be*?

The bride is the daughter of seriously rich bond trader Tyler August Waldorf, now deceased, and society hostess Mirabel Antoinette Kattrel Waldorf, also deceased. She has two children, Blair Cornelia Waldorf, who is seventeen today, and Tyler Hugh Waldorf, eleven. The groom is the son of Jeremiah Leslie Rose, former rabbi of Scarsdale Synagogue, now deceased, and Lynne Dinah Bank, a retired interior decorator, who resides in Mexico. His son, Aaron Elihue Rose, is seventeen.

After an absurdly short engagement, the two were married today. The couple chose the United Nations all-faiths chapel for the ceremony, since he is Jewish and she is Protestant and neither wanted to convert. The reception is going on as we speak at the swish St. Claire Hotel on East Sixty-first Street. Dinner includes a dish called quenelle, which is a fish mousse and is quite likely to make you very sick if you mix it with too much champagne. The couple will honeymoon on a yacht in the Caribbean for a month, leaving their children to fend for themselves at home while they are gone.

Hmm. That should get interesting!

The bride has taken the groom's surname, as has her son, Tyler. Her daughter, Blair, remains undecided. "No effing way," was her response when last asked.

Both the bride's and the bridegroom's previous marriages ended in divorce. It was all very scandalous at the time, but three cheers for them—they've moved on.

Better get back to the party!

You know you love me,

gossip girl

cheek to cheek

"I hope he's waiting for us in the lobby," Jenny said nervously.

"Don't worry," Vanessa soothed. "We'll find him."

They pushed their way through the St. Claire Hotel's revolving door and glanced around the sumptuous lobby. Both girls were dressed in the little black '60s dresses they'd picked up for ten dollars at Domsey's in Williamsburg. Jenny's was embroidered with jet beads, and Vanessa's had a velvet cat sewn into the skirt. She was also wearing black fishnet stockings, which was a first.

Both girls looked very retro and extremely cute.

"There he is!" Jenny squealed, making a beeline for Nate, who was sitting stiffly on a chair in the corner, gulping his champagne.

"Good," Vanessa said, suddenly feeling completely out of place. What was she supposed to do while Jenny and her rich preppy boyfriend were groping each other's asses? "I'll see you guys over at the bar."

She'd insisted that she was only coming along for moral support, but of course she had an ulterior motive. There was a chance Dan would pass by on his way to the bathroom or something. Then she wouldn't feel like she'd wasted her time putting on a dress.

★   ★   ★

"Hey, Jennifer," Nate said, kissing Jenny on the cheek and taking her hand.

"Hey," Jenny said, her eyes wide with excitement. She took in Nate's shiny lace-up shoes. His crisp black tuxedo. His wavy, golden-brown hair. His glimmering green eyes. "You look . . . really, really good."

Nate smiled. "Thanks. So do you."

"So what do you want to do?" she asked.

"Let's just sit down and hang out for a while, okay?"

"Okay," Jenny said. Nate led her over to a loveseat in a quiet corner by the bar.

"Is it okay if I just have a seltzer or something?" Jenny asked, crossing her legs and nervously uncrossing them again. "I feel kind of weird."

"Sure," Nate said. The waiter approached and he ordered for them. "Two seltzers."

Wow, he really *was* reforming.

He took Jenny's hand again and put it in his lap. Jenny giggled. It felt weird to be in a hotel bar with Nate instead of in the park or at his house. She felt like everyone in the hotel was watching them.

"Don't be nervous," Nate said quietly. He lifted her small hand and kissed the back of it tenderly.

"I'm trying not to be," Jenny said. She closed her eyes, took a deep breath, and leaned her head against Nate's shoulder. It was easy to relax when she was with Nate. He made her feel so safe. She opened her eyes to find Nate smiling down at her, his green eyes shining.

"I have a feeling I'm going to get in a lot of trouble for this," he said, as if he was looking forward to it.

Jenny frowned. "How come?"

"I don't know," Nate said. He wasn't about to explain to

Jenny that his girlfriend, Blair, was in the next room, probably armed and dangerous. "I just have a feeling," he said.

Jenny gave his hand a squeeze. "Don't worry," she said. "We're not doing anything wrong."

"So," Blair's mother said, when Cyrus had finished his speech and the quenelle and organic leaf salad were served. "Cyrus and Tyler and I have been talking about our name."

"What about our name?" Blair said. She poked her quenelle with her fork. "What is this stuff, anyway?"

"Don't you remember?" her mother said. "We chose it at the tasting."

Blair took a tiny bite. "It tastes like cat food," she said. She shoved her plate to the side and picked up her champagne glass.

"Anyway," her mother continued. "Tyler's agreed to change his name to Rose. And I've already done it. So that leaves you, Blair."

Blair kicked her chair leg. This wasn't the first time the subject had come up. "You're changing yours?" she asked her brother incredulously.

Tyler nodded. "I decided to, yeah. *Tyler Rose*. It sounds cool, doesn't it? Like a DJ or something."

"Definitely," Aaron agreed. He lowered his voice. "Laying on the phat beats it's Tyler Rose, coming to you live from Seventy-second Street."

"Shut up," Blair mumbled. As if her middle name weren't lame enough, now they were trying to stick her with an even lamer new last name? *Blair Cornelia Rose*—no fucking way. "I told you before. I'm not changing it," she said.

Her mother's face fell. "Oh, Blair. It'd be so nice if we all shared a name. Like a real family."

"No," Blair insisted.

Cyrus gave her a sympathetic smile. "It would mean a lot to me and your mother if you'd at least think about it some more," he said.

Blair pressed her lips together to keep from screaming in outrage. What part of "no" didn't they understand? She turned around to look for Nate, but his chair was . . . *empty*. Oh, why was everything such a fucking mess?

"Sorry," she said bitterly. The quenelle rose up in her throat, mingling fizzily with the liters of champagne she'd already consumed. Blair clapped her hand over her mouth and quickly fled the table.

Serena and Erik were making food sculptures with their quenelle. It was too nasty to eat, and the band hadn't started playing yet, so there was nothing else to do. Erik had stolen Nate's plate, and they'd stuck the three fish-shaped quenelles on top of each other, linking them together with two cocktail straws. Erik knew how to do this because he was studying architecture at Brown.

Dan actually liked the quenelle. He ate it very slowly, gathering courage for what he was about to do.

"Hey, can I talk to you for a minute?" he finally asked Serena, putting his hand on the table beside her plate to get her attention.

"Sure," she said, turning around.

"Don't mind me," Erik said, sandbagging their quenelle stack with balls of butter. "I've got work to do."

"What's up?" Serena said. She tucked her hair behind her ears and leaned toward Dan, giving him her complete attention.

Dan looked into her nearly navy blue eyes and tried to find what he was looking for. Something that would tell him he'd been silly to worry. That she loved him just as much as he loved her. He couldn't see anything but blue.

"I just wanted to say that I didn't mean to . . . I didn't want . . . when I sent you that poem, I thought . . ." Dan didn't know what he was trying to say. It sounded like he was apologizing, and he wasn't sorry. He wasn't sorry about anything but the fact that Serena's eyes were still blue, and nothing more.

"Oh, don't worry about it," Serena said. She took a sip of her champagne and fidgeted with the edge of the tablecloth. "You were just a little too intense, that's all," she added.

Too intense? Dan wondered. *What was that supposed to mean?*

All of a sudden the jazz band began to play.

"Oh, I love this song!" Serena cried. It was "Cheek to Cheek." She was a sucker for corny music.

"Ladies and gentlemen, the bride and groom!" the bandleader announced. Cyrus and Eleanor Rose stood up and twirled out onto the dance floor, beckoning to their guests to join them.

Chuck grabbed both Kati and Isabel's hands and twirled them away, his hands sliding down their backs to their butts within seconds.

"Want to dance?" Serena asked Dan. She stood up and held out her hand.

Dan looked up at her with hurt eyes, feeling very intense indeed. "No, thanks," he said. He stood up to leave. "I think I'll go smoke a cigarette."

Serena watched him go. She knew Dan was upset, but what could she do? It seemed like no matter what she said or did he would always find a reason to be miserable. That was the way he liked it. It gave him something to write about.

Serena preferred to be carefree and happy-go-lucky, just like her brother. She downed her champagne and grabbed Erik by the shoulders to distract him from his food games.

"Can't a girl have any fun anymore?" she asked him, giggling a little desperately.

Erik stood up. "This girl definitely can," he said, taking her in his arms and dipping her backward dramatically.

And it was true. Serena *did* always find a way to have fun, she just hadn't found it yet tonight. But the night was still young. . . .

amor omnia vincit—love conquers all

"Have you seen my brother?" Jenny asked Nate. "Is he having a good time?"

Nate flicked open his silver Zippo lighter and lit a cigarette. "I wasn't really paying that much attention," he admitted.

"I'm sure he is," Jenny said. She looked around at the hotel's decadent décor. "I mean, how could he not?"

Nate tilted his golden head and blew smoke at the ceiling. Jenny took a sip of her seltzer. "Are *you* having a good time?" she asked.

Nate leaned forward and rested his head on her bare shoulder. She smelled like baby powder and Finesse hair conditioner. "I'm having a much better time now than I was in there," he said.

"Really?" Jenny still couldn't get over the fact that Nate even liked her. Now he was telling her he'd rather hang out with her than be dancing at the reception of one of the biggest weddings of the year?

Nate ducked his head and kissed his way up the side of her neck and along her jawbone until he reached her lips. Jenny squeezed her eyes shut and kissed him back. She felt like a princess in a fairy tale, and she never wanted to wake up.

Dan slipped into a seat at the end of the St. Claire Hotel bar and ordered a double scotch on the rocks. With trembling hands he pulled a Camel out of his coat pocket and lit it. Tears fell on the cigarette's paper as it hung, damp and bent, from between his lips. He grabbed a pen from off the bar and drew a big black *X* on his cocktail napkin. It was all he could muster.

All those lovely, tragic poems he'd written had been meant to ward away the actual tragedy, the actual idea even, that Serena didn't love him. But it was true after all. She didn't.

The funny thing was, he wasn't crying over *her* so much as what she'd said.

He was too intense. A loser destined to scare people off because no one would be able to match his intensity.

Dan's chest convulsed in a sob and he slumped forward, resting his forehead against the edge of his glass. Out of the corner of his eye, he saw a familiar shock of curly brown hair, the enormous cleavage, the tiny figure.

His sister.

And next to her, with his hands all over her enormous cleavage and tiny figure was that rich bastard, Nate.

Dan really wasn't in the mood to watch his little sister get molested by some stoned Wasp with hash for brains. Sitting up, he poured the glass of scotch down his throat and spun around.

After throwing up her quenelle, Blair had gone outside to smoke a cigarette and get some fresh air. That didn't last long. It was November and she was freezing her ass off, so she went inside and headed back to the ladies' room to spruce herself up.

As soon as she rinsed out her mouth, smoothed down her hair, put on another coat of M•A•C Spice lipstick, and spritzed herself with perfume, she was going to find Nate and take him upstairs to their suite. Enough was enough. It was *her* birthday and she wanted it *her* way.

But as she passed through the bar on the way to the ladies' room, Blair stopped dead. In the corner, Nathaniel Archibald— *her* Nate—was kissing a little ninth-grade girl from Constance Billard.

The soundtrack came to a crescendo and then stopped dead. The leading lady trembled, her eyes wide.

Blair felt like she'd been shot in the stomach. Nate looked completely relaxed and happy. He and the girl—what was her name, *Ginny? Judy?*—were holding hands. They were smiling and murmuring sweetly to each other. They looked like they were in love.

This was definitely not in the script.

And as she looked on in horror and fascination, Blair had the most starkly disappointing realization of her entire life. Worse even than the thought of not getting into Yale.

Nate wasn't her leading man. He wasn't going to sweep her off her feet and love her and only her. He was just a supporting actor, some loser who would drop off the screen before the final act. And if that was the case, she definitely didn't want him.

Blair turned away, tears of disappointment clouding her vision as she headed into the ladies' room for the third time. She was badly in need of a cigarette, and she wanted to smoke it somewhere warm and private.

★ ★ ★

"Get your fucking hands off my sister," Dan growled, waving his burning Camel at Nate.

"Dan?" Jenny said, sitting up. "Don't. It's fine."

"It's not fine," Dan sneered at his little sister. "You don't know anything."

Nate gave Jenny's leg a reassuring squeeze and stood up. He reached for Dan's shoulder and patted it gently. "It's okay, man. We're friends. You know that."

Dan shook his head. Angry tears dripped off his face and onto the marble floor. "Get away from me."

"What's your problem?" Jenny demanded, standing up. "Are you drunk?"

"Come on, Jenny," Dan said, grabbing her arm. "Let's go home."

Jenny twisted out of his grasp. "Ow. Let go!" she cried.

"Hey, man," Nate said. "Why don't *you* go home? I'll make sure Jennifer gets home okay."

"Yeah, I'm sure you will," Dan spat. He lunged for Jenny's arm again.

"Yo, Dan," a girl's calm, sarcastic voice called from the bar. "Why don't you just go write a poem about it or something? You need to chill the hell out."

Dan, Jenny, and Nate looked up. It was Vanessa, perched on a bar stool in her black cat dress. Her lips were painted dark red. Her brown eyes were laughing. Her head was shaved like an army dude's. Her skin was so pale it gleamed. She looked pretty fabulous.

At least to Dan.

The most amazing thing was her eyes. Why had he never noticed them before? They weren't just brown like Serena's had been just blue. They were talking to him. And they were saying things that he wanted to hear.

"Hey," Vanessa said, speaking only to Dan.

"Hey," Dan said back. "What are you doing here?"

Vanessa slid off her stool and walked over. She put her arm around Dan's shoulders and kissed him on the cheek. "Buying you a drink," she said. "Come on."

as usual *b* is in the bathroom, but so is *s*

After "Cheek to Cheek," the band played "Putting on the Ritz." Serena and Erik pretended they were Ginger Rogers and Fred Astaire, camping it up in their corner of the dance floor. Serena swung her arms gaily, trying to be carefree, the life of the party. But she couldn't stop thinking about the hurt expression on Dan's face.

Then Chuck cut in.

"May I?" he asked, slithering his pinky-ringed hand around Serena's waist and butting Erik out of the way.

Serena couldn't have asked for a better reason to stop dancing. "No way," she said.

She walked off the dance floor and grabbed her purse from her chair. Maybe she could catch Dan at the bar and reason with him over cigarettes.

But when she got to the bar, Serena found that Dan was already being reasoned with . . . by Vanessa. Her arm was around him, and even though her head was still shaved and she was still wearing her Doc Martens, her face looked softer and sweeter than Serena had ever seen it. That was because Vanessa was looking at Dan and Dan was looking back at her and they were . . . *in love!*

Serena kept on walking, right into the ladies' room. She still wanted a cigarette, and she didn't want to ruin their moment.

Blair was perched on a sink at the far end of the bathroom, chain-smoking Merits. She heard someone come in, but she didn't turn her head. She was too wrapped up in her own tragedy.

There was a good chance she wasn't getting into Yale, even after her father's embarrassingly outrageous donation. Nate didn't love her. She didn't even have the same last name as the rest of her family anymore. And she was still a virgin. It was as if she really had become someone else without even trying. As if she'd been run over by a car and gotten amnesia and had gone on living without even realizing she'd been in an accident.

Blair's nose dripped on her dress and she swiped at it. She couldn't even tell if she was crying anymore. She felt numb.

"Hey, Blair, you okay?" Serena called out, a little timidly. Blair didn't actually have fangs, but she could still bite your head off.

Blair looked over her shoulder and nodded. Strands of brown hair were plastered to her wet cheeks, and her eyeliner was smudged.

"Here," Serena said, walking up and handing her a wad of paper towels. "I have some extra makeup and stuff in my purse if you need something."

"Thanks," Blair said, taking the paper towels. She blew her nose, her shoulders shaking with the effort. Serena had never seen her look so spent.

"Are you okay?" she asked again.

Blair looked up and saw genuine concern in Serena's blue eyes. It was unbelievable, but it was true. Even after Blair had been so incredibly mean to her, Serena still cared.

"No," Blair admitted. "I'm definitely not okay." Her chest heaved as she let out a sob. "My life is a mess."

One of the beaded shoulder straps on Blair's dress fell down. Serena reached out and put it back in place. "I saw you steal those pajama bottoms from Barneys," she said.

Blair looked up. "You didn't tell anyone though, did you?" she asked.

Serena shook her head. "Promise."

Blair sighed and looked down at her beautiful shoes. "I don't know why I did it," she said, her lower lip trembling. "He didn't even thank me for them."

Serena shrugged "Fuck 'em," she said. She dug around in her purse and pulled out a brush and a pack of cigarettes. She lit two cigarettes and handed one to Blair. "It's your birthday," she said.

Blair nodded and took the cigarette. She puffed tentatively on it as tears dripped down her face. And then she hiccupped, loudly.

Serena tried hard not to laugh, but she couldn't help it. Blair just looked so pathetic. She bit her notorious lips to hold back the giggles. Tears streamed down her perfect cheeks.

Blair glared at Serena. But when she opened her mouth to say something nasty, all that came out was another enormous hiccup. She sucked in her breath. "Fuck it," she giggled.

And once she started she couldn't stop. Neither could Serena. It felt so good to laugh! Mascara ran down their faces and their noses dripped on the floor, making them laugh even harder.

When they finally got control of themselves, Serena stood behind Blair and began brushing her hair. "Well, happy birthday," she said, looking at Balir in the mirror, her cigarette propped between her teeth. "Tell me if it hurts."

Blair closed her eyes and let her shoulders drop. For once, she wasn't thinking about her Yale interview, or losing her virginity to Nate, or her messed-up family. She wasn't the star of any movie. She was just breathing, enjoying the gentle tug and pull of the brush on her hair.

"It doesn't hurt," she told her old friend. "It feels good."

who left the party and who joined it

"I don't think Vanessa is going to want to leave with me," Jenny whispered to Nate, nodding to where Vanessa and Dan had their heads bent together at the bar.

"Who said you were leaving?" Nate asked.

Jenny smoothed her dress down over her thighs. She and Nate had been kissing for a while, and it had ridden up. "Well, don't you have to get back to the wedding reception? I mean, you are like, an usher and everything."

Nate tipped back his glass and crunched an ice cube between his teeth. He didn't care anymore who saw them together. Even Blair. He wanted them to see. "Yeah, but I'm taking you with me," he said.

"No way," Jenny gasped, half terrified and half thrilled to death. "I can't!"

But of course she was dying to go. She might even get her picture in *Vogue*!

"Come on," Nate said. He stood up and held out his hand. "Let's dance."

Dan took a big gulp of scotch and set his glass down on the bar. "So I bet you think I'm a total loser, right?" he said, turning to gaze into Vanessa's laughing brown eyes. Again, he wondered how he could have overlooked them.

"Well, you *are* a loser," Vanessa said, crossing her legs like a lady. She grabbed a handful of nuts from a dish on the bar and shoved them into her mouth.

"But you still love me, right?" Dan said, watching her intently.

Vanessa picked a ball of lint off her fishnets and flicked it onto the bar floor. She couldn't believe she was actually flirting with Dan. She hadn't even broken up with Clark yet! But it was kind of fun to be such a slut.

She leaned forward and kissed Dan on his quivering lips. "Right," she said, her mouth still full of nuts.

"Nate and I were supposed to have sex in here tonight," Blair said, flopping onto the bed in her hotel suite and kicking off her shoes. Her limbs were loose and floppy with exhaustion. It felt good to sprawl out.

Serena decided not to rub it in by asking Blair what had gone wrong. She pulled her dress off over her head and tossed it into an armchair in the corner. Wearing only her skimpy white satin La Perla underpants, she walked into the bathroom and put on a fluffy white terrycloth robe. She came out carrying an extra robe for Blair.

Blair took the robe and wriggled out of her dress. "Don't look," she warned. "I'm not wearing any underwear."

Serena laughed and rolled her eyes toward the ceiling. She'd forgotten about Blair's tendency to take things to extremes. "Don't tell me. You got a Brazilian wax, too, right?"

Blair smiled. Serena knew her too well. "Yeah, I did," she admitted. "What a waste." She tossed the dress onto the floor. "And that fucking thing was giving me a rash."

Serena walked over to the TV and clicked it on. "I wonder if they get the Playboy channel here. We could watch pornos and order beer from room service," she joked. She carried the remote over to the bed and sat down.

"Give me that." Blair grabbed the remote out of Serena's hand. "It's *my* birthday." If she wasn't going to have sex, she could at least watch American Movie Classics. They always played Audrey Hepburn movies. "Let's watch a movie and then go out to a club or something."

"Fine," Serena said, piling up the bed pillows so she could lean against them. "But can we order a pizza or something? I'm *starving*."

Blair scooted back on the bed so she was sitting right next to Serena. She clicked through the channels until she found AMC. *Breakfast at Tiffany's* was only just getting started. She settled in to watch, leaning her head back against the pillows until it was resting only inches away from Serena's, strands of her long brown hair mingling with Serena's blond ones.

The two girls watched Audrey Hepburn flit around her apartment and flirt with her new neighbor. They sang along as she sang "Moon River" out on her fire escape, and counted how many crazy hats she wore.

Audrey Hepburn was poised and thin and always knew what to say. She had incredible clothes and was fabulously beautiful. She was everything Blair wanted to be.

Blair sighed heavily. "I don't really look anything like Audrey, do I?" she asked out loud.

Serena smiled, keeping her eyes on the screen. "Sure you do," she said. And Blair decided to believe that what she said was true.

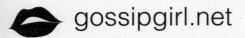
gossipgirl.net

Disclaimer: All the real names of places, people, and events have been altered or abbreviated to protect the innocent. Namely, me.

hey people!

Sightings

Late Saturday night: *D* and *V* holding hands as they left the St. Claire. Hey, doesn't she have a boyfriend? *J* and *N* riding around **Central Park** in one of those horse-drawn carriages. Cheesy, but cute. *B* and *S* at **Patchouli** downtown, dancing like wild things in their matching dresses. Sunday: *S* retrieving a wrapped package from *N*'s house. Later, *S* and *B* in **Barneys'** men's department, slipping a pair of cashmere pj bottoms back on the hanger. What good Samaritans!

Your E-Mail

Hey Gossip Girl,
First of all, you kick ass. Second of all, don't worry about B. Her mom and stepdad are going away for a month on their honeymoon, and we're all going to party like wild monkeys at her house. I should know, I live there too. ;)
—DoubleA

Dear DoubleA,
Who said I was worried? See you there!
—GG

Questions and answers

With everyone changing partners right and left it's kind of hard to know what will happen next!

Will *B* and *S* stay friends?

Will *B* and *N* become "just friends"?

Will **B** find true love? Will she lose it?

Will **V** ditch her boyfriend to be with **D**?

Will **D** be happy? Will he stop writing poetry?

Will **N** and **J** stay together?

Will **S** meet someone who can keep her attention for more than five minutes?

Will **I** ever stop talking about all of the above?

No way.

Until next time.

You know you love me,

gossip girl

Scandal. Intrigue. Deception.
What else are friends for?

Be sure to read all the Gossip Girl novels,
and keep your eye out for
Because I'm Worth It,
coming October 2003.